P9-DCL-773

IVAN
and the
informer

The Property of
The Bloomingrove Reformed Church

ivan
and the informer

MYRNA GRANT

Tyndale House
Publishers, Inc.
Wheaton, Illinois

The Property of
The Bloomingrove Reformed Church

Illustrated by
Jos. E. DeVelasco

Library of Congress
Catalog Card Number 76-58129
ISBN
0-8423-1846-1, paper

Copyright © 1974
and 1977
Tyndale House
Publishers, Inc.,
Wheaton, Illinois.
All rights reserved.

First Tyndale printing,
May 1977.
Printed in the
United States of America.

For Chris,
Sue, Drew,
and Jenni
with love
and appreciation

contents

◆The threat

Ivan Nazaroff strode along the snow-filled Moscow street, trying hard to pretend that nothing had happened. Behind him, he could hear the running footsteps of his sister, Katya. Her heavy boots were thudding through snow that had been falling all day and was swirling like clouds of smoke around the hunched and hurrying people.

"Ivan! Wait for me!"

Ivan wondered how many times he had heard that call. Sometimes it was tiresome to be always waiting for a ten-year-old sister, two whole years younger than he. Today it was worse than tiresome. He wanted to think.

Katya's face was bright with cold as she laid a thickly-gloved hand on Ivan's coat sleeve to steady herself and catch her breath. "The bus was so crowded, I almost missed getting off," she gasped. "Didn't you wonder where I was?"

Ivan marched on ahead, hoping his sister would not notice that he was upset. "Certainly not. You're much too old to have a brother leading you around. Besides, I saw you shoving your way off the bus."

Katya glanced quickly at her brother's stern face. "Why was Boris Petrovich waiting for you after school today?" She asked the question with a stab of fear. She knew Boris had just had his fifteenth birthday and was a new member of the Komsomol, the communist youth organization.

A gust of wind flung itself at the children, making them stagger against its force. Ivan fought ahead, pushing out his anger at Boris. He was grateful that the wind made it impossible to answer Katya.

But the turning of the corner gave them relief from the wind, and Katya, with her usual persistence, repeated the question.

"Same as always," Ivan finally answered. "He knows I am a Christian. He likes to make fun of me."

"But it wasn't the same," Katya retorted, her eyebrows tense with concern. "I saw him pushing you. He's a bully."

Ivan sighed. Katya had a way of persisting in her questions until she finally got the whole story, no matter what. "He said that as a Komsomol member he has a responsibility to convince me that Christianity is old-fashioned superstition. I told him I didn't have to listen to him, but he thinks he can make me."

"How will he make you?" The wind almost carried off Katya's words. "He can't *make* you listen!"

Ivan was trying not to think about it, let alone talk about it. But Katya's glance was insistent. "He's on the hockey team. The others know I am a believer and say nothing. The coach knows, but he is interested in a good team and I am a good player. But if Boris protests my being on the team, the coach will have to remove me. After all, the team is for the Young Pioneers, and believers don't belong to that!"

"But you have worked so hard! And it is such an honor to be chosen for the team. He's horrid!" Katya flung the words out with such indignation that an old woman, bent double as she slowly shoveled snow, stiffly raised her head and glanced briefly at Katya.

"We had an argument. I walked away. He would have come after me, but his bus was coming. He said he would be waiting for me after school tomorrow. He means to fight me."

Ivan pulled open the heavy door of the apartment building for his sister. It was a great relief to be in the long hallway and out of the wind and snow. He spoke quietly. "Say nothing of this to Momma, Katya. We don't want to worry her."

The wonderful smell of borscht greeted them as they entered their apartment.

"Momma, we're home!" Katya called, pulling off her boots with stiff fingers. Ivan sat down at the large table in the center of the living room, smiling as his mother bent to kiss him.

"What a cold day, children!" she exclaimed. "I have some hot tea ready for you. Katya, get the pot from the kitchen, please, and I'll bring out the glasses."

Ivan was glad this was a day his mother was home early from her job at the factory. He liked to smell the thick borscht soup already hot and to watch her steady hands laying out glasses and spoons and pouring the tea.

The children sat quietly, breathing the steam from the hot tea and feeling it warm their icy faces. Mother sat at the table

with them, mending silently and smiling when she glanced at the two children. Katya sipped her tea slowly. She wanted to make it last, but Ivan was already beginning his homework, his glass set carefully beside his book.

It would be at least an hour, Ivan knew, before Father returned from his factory job, and in that hour Ivan could get a good start on what he had to complete for school tomorrow.

A good feeling settled upon Ivan. The threats of Boris seemed far away. The tension of being the only believer in his classroom, the only one not to wear proudly the red neck scarf of the communist Young Pioneers, seemed eased. What if the others made fun of him? Here in this room, with the tea still warming him and the quiet face of his mother bending over her sewing, the difficulties at school subsided. Ivan raised his head from his book to smile at Katya. He was sorry he had been so irritated with her after school. But as he glanced up, the soft lace curtains at the window across the room suddenly lifted as a blast of cold air swept in from the open front door. He turned in his chair with astonishment.

◆Poppa in trouble

"Poppa! What are you doing home so early from your job?" Ivan jumped to his feet and anxiously took his father's heavy coat and hung it on the hook by the door.

"Poppa, are you sick?" Ivan persisted. Poppa sank wearily into his chair.

"Oh, no, son! I am not sick." He smiled to relieve the family's concern. "It's nothing so bad. I was asked to leave my job at the factory. I am to report to the supervisor in the morning."

Momma's voice was filled with dismay. "But why?"

Poppa shrugged. "Last week, one of the men beside me on the assembly line was asking me about Christian beliefs. It was a wonderful conversation."

"But Sergei, you know you must not speak about religion at the factory."

"I was answering his questions. That is

permitted by our Soviet law."

Katya burst out indignantly, "It is *supposed* to be permitted."

"He was my friend."

Momma went to the window and stared out. The room was quiet. "Believers cannot trust friends in Russia." The children could hear a tinge of weariness in her voice. "So often such people are only police informers, wanting to cause trouble."

The face of Boris Petrovich suddenly appeared in Ivan's mind. A tight feeling of fear returned to his chest, and he looked down at his school book still open on the table.

"We have other believers for friends, Momma," Ivan reminded her gently.

Momma turned from the window with a smile. "Of course! This is not so bad. Your father will have an opportunity in the morning to explain to the supervisor that he was only answering his comrade's questions." Momma gave Poppa a warm hug.

Poppa pulled Momma to the chair beside him and held her hand. "It is good for us to pray about all this."

Ivan and Katya nodded eagerly and

bowed their heads as Poppa began.
"Thanksgiving and praise to Almighty God
that I am counted worthy to bear this
small concern for the sake of Jesus.
Praise for the love of God, that can reach
even to my supervisor. Praise for the
forgiveness of God, that can give new life to
the worker who reported me."

A feeling of sweetness touched Ivan,
as it had many times before in prayer.

"Bring glory to the name of Jesus,"
Momma prayed.

Ivan silently agreed, and within himself
he added, *Even through me, Lord, if You
want. Even through me.*

Momma gave Katya a playful spank.
"Come! Let us set the table for supper!"

"Yes! Borscht!" Ivan declared
enthusiastically. "It smells so good,
Momma."

Poppa inhaled deeply. "It's the best in
Moscow, Ivan. Your momma made it."

"I peeled the beets!" Katya shook out
the tablecloth. "And I went to the shop
especially for the sour cream. You should
have seen all the lines today. It was no
fun, I tell you! Waiting all that time just for
sour cream!"

Poppa tugged teasingly at the bow that

caught Katya's two brown braids in a pretty loop at the back of her head. "Someday you will be as fine a cook as your momma, Katychka. Keep peeling the beets!"

They all laughed, Ivan louder than the rest.

It had been cold all day in the classroom, and Ivan wrapped his sweater tightly around himself and folded his arms, hugging himself for warmth. Usually he loved history, but today it was hard to listen to his teacher, Sophia Kutskova. His mind was on his father's factory and what had happened at Poppa's meeting with the supervisor. Sophia Kutskova was talking about the examinations which she had just handed back.

"Our leader, Lenin, would have been proud of your work, students. You have mastered some rather lengthy sections of Soviet history, and I, too, am pleased. It is important that you be able to follow the development of all that went into our glorious revolution."

The clock on the wall reminded Ivan that in a few minutes, school would be over, and perhaps he would have to confront Boris. He tried harder to concentrate on what his teacher was saying.

"In a very few years, many of you students will be proud to be in the Komsomol." Sophia Kutskova's eyes rested for an instant on Ivan, then moved away. "You will be happy, then, to have studied so diligently. Your history will mean even more to you when you all take your places in the service of your country in the Young Communist League." She paused. "Now you are dismissed."

Ivan gathered his books up quickly. *If only Katya is ready, perhaps we can hurry and avoid Boris,* he thought. He was startled to hear his teacher calling his name.

"Ivan Nazaroff, stay back. I wish to speak to you."

Ivan hurried to the front of the room. His teacher smiled as she beckoned him to sit down. She glanced at the open grade book on her desk. "You did well on your history examination."

Ivan returned his teacher's smile. "Thank you, Sophia Kutskova. I like history very much."

"I confess, I do not understand your

behavior." The teacher looked suddenly grave.

Ivan felt a pang of guilt. He tried to think what he could have done.

"You excel in history," Sophia Kutskova continued. "I sense in you a deep stirring of love for Mother Russia. And yet you will not wear the red neck scarf that shows you to be a loyal communist Young Pioneer."

"I'm sorry, Sophia Kutskova."

"We have talked together many times. You understand so much, Ivan. It makes me sorry to see you stubborn and set against me."

Ivan flushed. A flutter of fear tightened his voice. "I am not against *you*, Sophia Kutskova."

"Your parents are lost in the past. If they were not, they would know how corrupt and imperialistic their religious ideas are. They are clinging ignorantly to ideas that were swept away with the czars. But you are young, Ivan, and have the possibility before you of a great education."

His teacher looked at Ivan expectantly. When he did not reply, she continued with a lecture Ivan had heard many times before, from many teachers.

"Why can you not see that you are throwing away your future for nothing? In years to come, no university will admit you if you cling to these fanatical ideas. I implore you to think about your future." Once again his teacher paused.

This time Ivan knew he must answer. "I do think about it, Sophia Kutskova."

The teacher smiled warmly. "Good. Then you will see that these uncultured ideas, this unscientific religious superstition, cannot be for a young and progressive Soviet youth like you. There is nothing ahead for you but trouble and suffering if you cling to religion."

She stood up, still smiling. Ivan stood also and picked up his books. "Thank you, Sophia Kutskova. I know you have my interests at heart."

The teacher laid her small hand on his shoulder. "Of course I do." She paused and looked warningly at him. "And do you think it is easy for me to have one student in my class, as late in the year as this, who still refuses to wear the red scarf?"

◆A new job

Ivan walked slowly, trying to make the short block between bus stop and home last as long as possible. Feelings of relief and dread were struggling in his mind.

He was relieved that Boris had not carried out his threat to fight him after school. Even the hockey practice today had been uneventful, although since Boris was the oldest boy on the team, his influence with the coach worried Ivan. And today Boris had seemed to make as much of that relationship as possible. Time and again he had skated up to the coach, resting his stiffly-gloved hand on the coach's shoulder, suggesting plays, making little jokes, or listening to some confidence of the coach and nodding his head in agreement. But nothing had been said about Ivan.

All the same, Ivan's steps were slow

with dread. Perhaps Boris and his threats were unimportant, but what had happened to his father today at the meeting with his supervisor was important!

There was no good smell of borscht today as Ivan opened the door of the apartment. The tearful face of Katya was the first thing he saw. Ivan's heart sank.

Her voice was thick from crying. "Ivan! Where have you been? Poppa has been at the police station all day. Momma went there when I got home from school, to see if she could find out anything." Katya hunched miserably in the corner of a big chair. Her schoolbooks were unopened on the table across the room.

"I was at hockey practice." Ivan unwound his knitted scarf and sat on the arm of Katya's chair.

"Everything is wrong, Ivan. I'm so worried about Poppa. And hardly anyone in my class will be friends with me. They think I am stupid to believe in God. I want to have friends like everyone else."

Ivan awkwardly handed her his handkerchief. "You have Christian friends," he offered, trying to be helpful.

"If I don't mind never seeing them!" Katya blew her nose loudly. "How often can we meet, anyway? It has to be someone's wedding or birthday or funeral, because believers have to get permission to meet in homes. I want to be with a lot of friends, all together, and without worrying about the police!" She blew her nose again and began to feel better.

Ivan was thinking that perhaps they ought to pray for Poppa, but before he could suggest it, the door swiftly opened and their parents hurried into the room, cold from the walk from the police station.

It had not been a bad time, really, Poppa said cheerfully. The police had asked why he was trying to influence fellow workers to become believers. Poppa had explained that he had only been answering his fellow worker's questions, and this was allowed by law.

Momma blew into the hot glass of pale tea that Katya had brought to warm her. "Then they brought the superintendent from the factory, and he accused your father of laziness and stealing!"

Poppa continued unlacing his heavy work boots. "We should laugh, Natasha. So many of the men take things from the factory—a small tool, or some wood. The superintendent himself has carried off enough supplies to begin a small shop of his own. And *he* tells the police that *I* have been stealing."

Momma's voice was unsteady. "And to think you have never stolen so much as a minute from the factory!"

"But what about your job, Poppa?" Ivan was impatient to get to the outcome.

"It's not so bad. Not nearly so bad as it could be. A new job, but I'll be home every night. I have been assigned to the State Collective Farm Number 46, outside of Moscow."

Katya jumped up and stamped her foot. Her dark eyes were flashing. "A farm worker! Oh! To do nothing wrong! To be honest and good, and to be punished! How glorious is our Mother Russia!"

Momma placed a firm hand on Katya's arm. "Katya! I have spoken to you before about this. You must guard your thoughts and your tongue. You know the danger in speaking carelessly."

But Katya was still angry. "Perhaps Ivan is an informer? You think he will tell what I said?"

"It is the habit of thought and speech that I fear," Momma replied sternly. "You must learn to discipline your thoughts!" She

stared at Katya as if she would say more and then sighed. "You children have homework to do, and I have supper to prepare. Let's talk no more about this."

Later that night, Ivan lay awake in bed. The moon shone through the lace curtains at the window. His parents had talked and prayed long into the night, and the drone of their voices had made him drowsy. But now they were silent, and Ivan propped himself up on his elbow and looked at the drifting moon.

It *was* unjust that his father, a trained factory worker, was assigned to a farm. His father had only answered a fellow worker's questions about Christianity. But the supervisor disliked believers and had chosen to report Poppa, and the police had chosen to pretend to believe the lie about Poppa's stealing. The police, the supervisor, and Poppa all knew that the real reason Poppa was being sent to the farm was to make life difficult for him because he was a believer.

Sophia Kutskova's words rang in Ivan's memory. *There is nothing ahead for you but trouble and suffering, if you cling to religion.*

The moon slipped behind a dense

cloud, plunging the room into darkness. A few faint stars, not visible before, came into view.

How strange that simply to believe in God could cause such troubles. For as long as he could remember, Ivan had known God existed. He could not imagine "changing his mind" to say that there was no God. A person had only to look at the sky to know the wonder of God's creation!

But commitment to Jesus had not come easily to Ivan. When he had become old enough to understand the cost of being a believer, he had been afraid. Life was too exciting, too full of possibilities, to choose a life that would close so many important doors. Ivan smiled at the emerging moon as he remembered his determination to resist the call of Jesus Christ. It seemed so long ago.

His conversion had been simple, really. Ivan remembered walking in the forest in the spring, in a world of green light and damp freshness. When he had gone into the forest, he had not been a Christian. When he had come out, he was. He tried to bring back what had happened to him in that walk, but it was a blur. His mind had been pulling in all directions; he remembered that. Then there had been a long time spent sitting against a tree. There had been an inner listening to some Bible verses Momma had taught him. There had been an inner argument, too. Then a warm sense of a Presence had come over him, and a word, "Come!" echoed in his heart. He had walked out of the forest with Christ. That part he remembered. And how Poppa had cried for joy! Poppa!

Ivan was fully awake now! How could he have lain, half-dreaming, forgetful of what awaited his father in the morning? Was it not a disgrace that a skilled factory worker would dig and carry on a farm? Poppa would have to leave Moscow on the earliest possible train and return to the apartment late. Was this not unjust? Ivan lay back on his pillow, staring at the ceiling. Morning would be a long time in coming.

◆A secret meeting

The argument had started slowly. Ivan had not meant to quarrel with Poppa. In fact, he had wanted to help him in some way. Ivan could see how tired and discouraged he was feeling after his first long day on the collective farm.

"Never mind, Natasha," Poppa had said to Momma. "Was not our Lord falsely accused? It is an honor to suffer for His sake."

It was not the words that had made Ivan feel a surge of love for his father. It was the playful way Poppa had smiled, as if comparing himself to the Savior were a gentle kind of joke.

Poppa had eaten his supper hungrily, but without talking. When it was over, he called Ivan away from the last pages of his homework, talking softly because Katya was already in bed.

"You were planning, son, on meeting some of your friends this Sunday?"

Ivan had answered happily. It was his friend Alexi's birthday, and a perfect time for a few Christian boys to gather at Alexi's home without raising suspicion. But Poppa had been hesitant.

"Perhaps it would be best, this time, not to go. My trouble with the police—"

Ivan could tell by Momma's face that she agreed. She was clearing away Poppa's dinner plate and paused to listen to the conversation.

"But Poppa! No! I promised I would go. It is the only chance we boys have to be together and talk freely as believers. They will think I am afraid if I don't go. They'll know you have been sent to the collective farm."

Poppa observed that it was not quite as important what one's friends thought as what the police thought. He explained again how careful Christians had to be not to draw attention to themselves in any way. But Ivan pleaded all the harder to be allowed to go. In the end, Poppa had given permission.

"Come in, Ivan! You're covered with

snow!" With the exuberance of a boy newly turned fourteen, Alexi flung open the door. His high cheekbones were flushed with color, and his fair hair had been carefully combed for the occasion.

"Happy birthday, Alexi!" Ivan embraced his friend warmly, in the Russian manner. "My mother sends these cookies."

"Thank you!" Alexi slammed the door hard, oblivious to the amusement of the other guests. "Off with your coat and boots, Ivan. You look frozen."

He held the cookies aloft, bearing them to the table with a flourish. Two boys, both older than Ivan, sat watching Ivan's entrance with smiles of pleasure. At the same time they followed with keen interest the path of the cookies through the air.

"These we shall have with tea," Alexi declared. "And the little cakes Mother made for us."

"A feast!" Pyotr Kachenko was tall for his age, and sturdy. "Good peasant stock" he said of himself with satisfaction, and whether it was his height or his peasant stock that provided him with an astonishing appetite, no one knew.

But Alexi whisked the cookies to a safe distance, placing them in front of Fyodor Sakovich. Fyodor was Pyotr's opposite. Small for fifteen, and slight of build, he was the pride of his family because of his athletic ability and excellent grades at school. With a grin, he pushed the cookies even farther down the table, away from Pyotr's enthusiasm, meanwhile greeting Ivan with a wave of his free hand.

Alexi emerged from the kitchen, carrying a small tea tray clinking with glasses. On a side table in the room sat a brass samovar, the family's prized possession. Its surface was beaded with steam from the scalding water inside. With gusto, Alexi began making the tea and handing the glasses to his friends.

"Looks more like a real birthday party this way! It's always best to be on the safe side, brothers!"

Ivan smiled at his friend. "It *is* a birthday party, Alexi. I do wish you many years to come."

The other boys added their greetings until Alexi was beaming with embarrassed pleasure and passing the cakes and cookies insistently, even though he had secretly

hoped to have some left over for bedtime.

Today, in preparation for the birthday, Alexi had copied down some Scripture from a recent overseas radio broadcast. With a flourish of triumph, he pulled a folded paper out of his pocket.

"This Scripture I have is from Jeremiah!" He opened the paper and laid it carefully on the table in front of him. "Some of it in the middle I missed, because Masha fell out of bed and made a great racket and I couldn't hear."

Pyotr threw back his head and laughed loudly. "Radios should come with ropes for tying up little sisters! In my case, *chains* for our Sonya!" The exploits of Pyotr's tiny sister were notorious. "But never mind, let's get on with what you have."

Soon the boys were absorbed in the words of Alexi's paper. Then they talked quietly together about what must be left behind when one follows Christ.

Pyotr's merry eyes became grave when he talked about his dream of continuing his piano lessons. "My teacher says I am good enough to play here in Moscow someday, if I could keep on. But of course, I am not a member of the Komsomol, so advanced lessons are impossible."

"It is sports that I miss." Fyodor spoke in a low voice. The boys knew how much gymnastics meant to him.

But Fyodor brightened and smiled with a shrug. "Once when I was small, I was in a physical culture show at Dynamo Stadium. That is something to remember! There were hundreds of us on the field, and when we finished, a great curtain of water jets shot to the sky. It was wonderful! But of course, the Organization of Sports Societies does not permit entrance to anyone not in the Komsomol. Now that I am fifteen and should have joined, that is over for me."

"But the Lord will repay you, Fyodor," Alexi reminded him softly.

"No question of that. But it is hard."

As the youngest boy in the group, Ivan said little. It was enough to be with Christian friends, feeling the warmth of their mutual affection and concerns. The awkward, tight feeling that sometimes closed in on him at school was completely gone. He loved to bend his head over the same paper that absorbed the other boys and join with them in prayer. Ivan wished the afternoon could go on forever.

It was Fyodor who had to leave first. They had finished their study and prayers, and were singing some of the church hymns their parents had taught them. Pyotr led enthusiastically.

As Fyodor prepared to leave, there was a flurry. Somehow Alexi had lost his paper with the Scripture among the empty glasses and plates on the table, or among the coats piled on the chairs. Fyodor helped to look for it as long as he could, but finally, cramming his gloves into his pockets and leaving his coat unbuttoned in his haste, he left with hurried apologies and more birthday wishes.

It was pleasant for the three other boys to sit together discussing school and their teachers and the hockey teams. Pyotr and Alexi thought Ivan should not worry about Boris and his threats. The coach had already shown that he wanted to overlook the fact that Ivan was not a member of the Young Pioneers. That should reassure him. And besides, Ivan was a very good player! Pyotr rumpled Ivan's hair affectionately. And it should not be too hard to stay away from Boris after school.

All too soon, the time came for Ivan to

go home. Pyotr had been invited to stay for supper with Alexi, and was already singing loudly as he began to help clear up the room before Alexi's parents returned from church. Ivan shrugged into his coat reluctantly. It had been a wonderful afternoon. His heart sang as he ran lightly down the apartment stairway to the front door.

If he had known what was waiting for him, he would not have been whistling as he opened the door and stepped out into the darkening street.

◆Police questioning

Ivan was intent on peering down the road to see if a bus was coming through the freezing Moscow twilight. At first he did not notice the two men moving out of a doorway toward him.

He began to run as the dim lights of the bus appeared, the cold snow creaking and snapping under his boots.

"Ivan Nazaroff?" Ivan was startled as the two figures squarely blocked his way. In an instant he knew they were members of the secret police. His heart pounded.

"Yes?" How could they know his name?

"Where are you coming from?"

Ivan's tongue seemed frozen in his mouth. The bus lumbered slowly past him, its headlights catching the three figures by the edge of the street, then moving on.

The taller of the two men, a disciplined, soldierlike figure, took Ivan's arm. "I am Comrade Grigory Yakov. You have some questions to answer, Ivan Nazaroff. We will go to the police station and see what we can discover."

Squeezed between the two officers in the back seat of the small police car, Ivan stared at the seat in front of him. He did not dare turn his head to look out of the wide windows. The tall policeman was sitting erect, glancing at his watch and out into the winter evening. The other officer had leaned his head against his window and appeared to be falling asleep. The driver of the car never turned to look at his passengers.

Ivan clenched his hands together in his lap in an effort to gather strength for what lay ahead. If only Poppa were with him! He pictured the scene at home: Katya setting the table and Momma bringing in the plates of bread and soup, perhaps glancing out the window to see if he were coming.

With eyes open, Ivan began to pray. It was hard to concentrate in the lurching car, as it slowed for intersections and then sped up. Ivan was anxious not to

appear to be praying. He tried to tighten the muscles in his face into a stern expression.

The car slid to a quiet stop. Comrade Yakov sprang out, holding the door for Ivan. The three walked briskly through the iron entrance gates and into the bright light of the police station. They entered a small room where the men began removing their coats. Ivan took his coat off as he was directed, hands shaking as he unbuttoned his coat.

Comrade Yakov sat down behind a small desk, pen in hand.

"Comrade Ivan Nazaroff, where were you this afternoon?" His voice was patient and not unfriendly.

"At a birthday party. At the home of Alexi Petrovich. I've done nothing wrong."

The second officer lazily lit a cigarette and stood in front of Ivan. "Yes. You were at the home of Alexi Petrovich. Perhaps it was his birthday. Perhaps it was something else, as well." He blew a puff of smoke toward the ceiling. "What did you do at the home of Alexi Petrovich?"

"We had a birthday party. We had tea and cookies that my mother sent, and cakes." It helped to be able to talk.

"And who else was at this home this afternoon?" The first officer raised his pen.

"It was a birthday party. Alexi Petrovich, my friend, was fourteen."

"Who else was present?" Comrade Yakov frowned. He did not like to repeat himself.

Ivan sat staring at the pen in Comrade Yakov's hand. If it were only a birthday party, why would he not tell the names of those present? To refuse would be to admit that something illegal had taken place. In a low voice he gave the names of his friends, insisting, "It was a birthday party."

But the interrogation was just beginning. A long line of questions followed, concerning his school, his father's job, his mother's job, the name of every friend he could remember, where his family had lived before coming to their present apartment, his teacher's name, his grades, his sister's grades, her friends. Ivan began to feel light-headed from the stuffy room and from hunger. He had not eaten supper, even if the police had. Did Ivan have a Bible? Did he know what Jeremiah meant? Did he ever attend church?

It seems that hours had passed, when the two men abruptly stood and left, locking the door of the small room behind them without explanation. As the door quickly opened and closed for the men, Ivan's heart lurched. He thought he glimpsed a boy in the hall—perhaps two boys.

After a long interval, the officers returned. They appeared pleased; there was a lightness in their manner, although their faces remained professionally severe. More questions followed, this time along a different and more alarming line.

Was it possible that his father was religious? What prayer-house* did his father attend? Was his mother a believer? Was he? His sister? The answers burned in his throat and he could feel trickles of perspiration down the sides of his face. Again the questions returned to the birthday party, and Ivan repeated the answers he had given earlier. There was a pause. Putting his hand inside his pocket, Comrade Yakov slowly pulled out the small piece of paper on which Alexi had written his verses from Jeremiah.

Ignoring the paper, and asking the

*Soviet term for church building.

questions as if he did not know the answer, Comrade Yakov leaned toward Ivan. "At this 'birthday party,' a paper was passed around. What was on the paper?"

Ivan's eyes reflected his horror at seeing the white paper in the officer's hand. Angrily, Comrade Yakov shouted the question again.

"Verses from Jeremiah." What would happen to him? He knew of older Christian boys who had been beaten by the police.

"What is that? What is Jeremiah?" The short officer was smoking again, and he spat out his words.

Suddenly Ivan could almost see his father as he looked when he came home from his interview at the police station only days earlier. Ivan remembered his words: "It is an honor to suffer for His sake." Ivan took a steadying breath.

"It is a part of the Bible, comrade. It is a part of the Old Testament."

There was a long pause. There was a stillness in the room that had not been there before. *Perhaps it is my own fears that are still,* Ivan thought. He had stopped trembling, and he raised a hand to push his wet hair off his forehead.

"That is all for the present. You may go home now." Comrade Yakov's voice seemed to boom out of a vacuum. Ivan could not believe what he was hearing. But the police left immediately, leaving the door open behind them as their footsteps rapidly faded down the hall.

A cold blast of air from the corridor made Ivan begin to shake. Quickly he pulled on his coat. The hall was dark and empty, and he hurried outside. From the appearance of the streets, Ivan knew it was late. Knees still shaking from his ordeal, he found his way to a subway station entrance, grateful that he still had his bus fare in his coat pocket. An old woman swabbing the subway platform with a filthy mop glanced at him in surprise. Ivan was sure, then, that it was very late.

◆Pytor's accusal

It seemed strange that life continued in the ordinary way the next day. The evening at the police station had been so extraordinary that somehow Ivan was surprised that the streets of Moscow were unchanged and that the hours at school passed as if nothing had happened to him at all.

Returning home so late the night before and seeing every window in his parents' apartment lit in the darkened building had given Ivan a peculiar sensation. Such a feeling of exhaustion had overcome him that it had been hard to force himself up the stairs, even though he was longing for food and bed and was eager to relieve his family's fears.

But today, in spite of an odd feeling of tiredness, all seemed as before.

Perhaps it was because Ivan was dozing

over his homework after school that he was so startled by Poppa's unusually early homecoming from work. Poppa seemed suddenly to be in the room, the door still open behind him. He laughed at their astonishment, swinging Katya in his arms and making her shriek with delight. He set Katya down and gave Momma a joyful hug. Bewildered, Ivan closed the door. His mind was hazy with sleep, but he knew it was much too soon for Poppa to be home from the collective farm.

Gathering the family to the table, Poppa laughed away their excited questions and began to explain. "This morning at the train station, as I was waiting to go to the farm with the other workers, a police car pulled up and the comrade officer called me over."

Ivan saw his mother's folded hands tighten.

"I was told to get in to be driven to the subway, where I could get transportation to my factory! I was told to return to my old job at the factory, and that is where I have worked all day."

Momma's eyes were wet. "Praise to our glorious God!"

"Yes!"

Smiles of joy remained on the family's faces throughout the evening. Katya finished her homework early enough to read a book before bedtime. Apparently all was well with the world.

Ivan tried not to think about the questions that were nagging at his brain. *Why was Poppa given his job back?* There was something about it that did not seem to fit. He tried to concentrate on his homework, but his train of thought was often interrupted by a flood of questions. All day he had watched at school for Alexi or Pyotr or Fyodor. He was worried that he had not seen any of them all day. *Were they not at school? Were they being held by the police? How had the police known about the meeting? How had they obtained the paper with the Bible verses?* His head swam and buzzed over his books, and then everything was quiet. From a long distance away he could hear Momma's voice.

"Ivan. No more homework! You must go to bed. You had so little sleep last night!" Poppa was helping him up from his chair and leading him to bed. Almost in a dream, he undressed and fell asleep.

Snow fell all the next day. The students in Moscow School Number 17 were accustomed to seeing it pile up on the sills of the narrow windows until it almost blocked their view of the sky. Ivan tried to shake off the questions that had worried him. Last night's sleep had greatly refreshed him, and the events of the Sunday night police questioning seemed unreal. Perhaps nothing more would come of it. Still, Ivan's eyes scanned the halls and courtyards for a glimpse of one of his Christian friends.

Sophia Kutskova praised Ivan as he gathered up his books for the day and slipped them into his schoolbag.

"I am happy to see you working so hard, Ivan." She smiled, her eyes resting on the collar of his shirt. He knew she was silently reminding him that he ought to be wearing the red neck scarf of the Young Pioneers.

"There is to be an all-Moscow intermediate history competition in the spring. Examinations will be given, and students with the best marks from all the schools will be asked to write a historical essay. You have the highest grade in our classroom, Ivan. I would like to choose you to represent our class, and indeed, the intermediate school." She hesitated. "Of course, I cannot select a student of history who does not proudly wear his own country's red scarf." There was a pleading in her eyes that made Ivan uncomfortable. "You could win for our school, Ivan. I know it. Over every other school in Moscow! Please think about what I am saying."

Ivan hurried along the hall. In a group of students ahead, Katya was chatting with a classmate. Ivan knew she would be so happy to have a friend that she would not want to ride the bus with him.

Outside, the wind stung his face, and he licked the snowflakes that fell on his lips. Some boys were sliding on the ice in the schoolyard, while others were throwing huge snowballs and shouting with laughter as the snowballs exploded softly on the coats of their classmates. Ivan heard his name called. It was Pyotr, pushing between students, his breath puffing a cloud in front of him as he ran, and his blond hair wet against his forehead.

A handful of snow Pyotr had scooped up as he ran hit Ivan softly on the chest, bursting in all directions in a spray of white.

"You want a snowball fight, do you, Pyotr Kachenko?" Ivan called with joy. Pyotr was beside him now, catching his breath and frowning. His voice was guarded.

"Stay over here a bit, away from the others. Keep the snowballs coming. I want to talk to you."

It would be safer, of course, if they were not seen together for too long. Pretending to have a snowball fight was a good idea, but Pyotr looked very upset as he told Ivan what had happened.

All the boys from Alexi's party had been taken that Sunday night to the police station. All had been questioned and finally released, Pyotr reported. Fines of fifty rubles each had been assigned to the parents of the boys, for permitting them to attend an "illegal youth meeting."

Ivan wondered why his parents had not been fined. Fifty rubles! That was a lot of money!

Pyotr was indignant about the paper with the verses from Jeremiah. How had the police obtained this? Ivan also wondered.

In a flash, his head seemed to clear. He understood the uneasy questions that had been nagging him since Sunday. An

informer! One of the boys would have to have told!

He could hardly bring himself to put the thought into words. Catching a gloveful of snow and tossing it, he stepped a little closer to Pyotr.

"Could there have been—an informer, Pyotr?"

Pyotr's expression did not change. He crossed his arms and thrust out his chin, observing Ivan carefully.

"I was going to ask you that question, Ivan."

Ivan stared in dismay at the accusing face of his friend.

He, the informer? Surely Pyotr couldn't think that he would do such a thing! Suddenly he felt as if he were with a stranger. He stammered as he spoke.

"But, Pyotr! You don't think it was *me?* Why-why would I do such a thing?"

The older boy's face remained unchanged. "I wonder how many rubles *your* family had to pay, Ivan." Seeing Ivan's confused expression, he continued sadly, "You told us on Sunday that your father had lost his job at the factory and had to do unskilled labor at the state collective farm. Yet everyone knows that now he has his old job back. Why would such a nice thing happen to your father, Ivan?"

Ivan could not bear the hurt expression on Pyotr's face. His eyes dropped to the snow at his feet as he answered, "I do not know, Pyotr Kachenko. But I promise you, it had nothing to do with me. You must not think I was the informer."

But the boots of Pyotr Kachenko were already moving swiftly away from Ivan. Pyotr had not waited for an answer.

◆A frightening visit

It would have been easier if Ivan had told his parents about Pyotr's accusation.

It would have been better, perhaps, but Ivan decided not to do it. His parents had enough worries of their own.

But it was hard. Only for an hour or two every day did Ivan forget that his friends believed he was an informer. Bent over his hockey stick, skimming the ice, slamming the puck to his teammates, Ivan thought of nothing except the game, the net, and the score. It was wonderful to have been chosen for the team, and an admiring glance from a teammate as he shot the puck or a word of encouragement from the coach pushed him into playing as never before.

Boris Petrovich was a brilliant goalie, moving constantly, crouching in the net, swaying from side to side, his eyes never leaving the puck. Soon the league games would begin. Boris was sure to be chosen. So far Boris had not made an issue of the fact that, as a Christian, Ivan belonged to no communist organization. But when the league games sponsored by the Komsomol began, would he then begin to complain?

In the locker room, Ivan watched him move from friend to friend, laughing, and making his way to the coach to tell some joke that brought an amused smile to the lips of the older man. Every other member of the school team was also a member of the Young Pioneers, or had just turned fifteen and joined the Komsomol. They knew each other well from the club meetings, and Ivan envied the boys' easy friendliness with one another. He threw his skates in his locker and quietly made his way out of the locker room and into the biting Moscow cold.

It seemed a long time since he had seen Alexi or Fyodor. He did not blame them for avoiding him, if they thought he was an informer. They had to be cautious. Their families had already been heavily fined. Why would they continue to be friends with a person who they thought had informed?

The wind wailed between the buildings. Ivan felt miserably alone. He had to tell someone!

Katya was curled up in Poppa's chair reading her geography notes. She was trying to memorize the major cities of the Ural mountains, and she barely looked up as Ivan flung himself into the apartment.

"Katya!"

She lowered her book, surprised by the urgent note in Ivan's voice.

"I've got to talk to you! I'm in trouble."

Katya's half smile faded into concern. She uncurled her legs and sat on the edge of Poppa's chair as Ivan drew up a wooden chair from the big table beside her.

"What trouble?"

"I can't tell Poppa and Momma. They have enough difficulties of their own. But something doesn't make sense."

Katya strained to follow the conversation.

"Poppa is fired from his job at the factory and told he must work as a farmer in the collective outside Moscow." His voice was thoughtful. "That Sunday I participate in a Christian meeting with my friends. Someone reports all of us. The next day, Poppa has his job back at the factory, and we are not even fined, although the other boys' families are. I don't understand."

Katya shook her head in impatience. "*I* don't understand what *trouble* you're in. Do you mean that questioning by the police?"

"No, it's not that...."

"Then what?"

Ivan still talked slowly, his eyes searching Katya's face for reactions.

"Someone informed. Right, Katya?"

"Yes!" Her voice was impatient.

"The boys think it was me," his words came in a rush, "so that Poppa could get back his job at the factory. They think I went to the police and confessed and offered their names because of Poppa."

Katya's expression froze.

"Your friends told you they think *you* are an *informer?*" Her shock melted into anger. "It is terrible that they could think such a thing!"

Ivan smiled at her loyalty. "No. It is logical. There was no other way for the police to discover that we were studying Scripture except through an informer." What he was saying suddenly chilled him

to the bone. "Katya! *I* am not the informer!
But one of the other boys *is!*"

The children sat in silence for a moment.
The enormity of the idea overwhelmed
them.

"The police had been given the piece of
paper with Scripture on it that we used at
the meeting. It had to be someone who had
been there. Katya, I've been so upset
about being accused of informing, I've
not wanted to face the fact that the real
informer has to be Pyotr, Fyodor, or
Alexi. But we have to admit this must be
true."

Katya looked bleak.

Ivan paced the floor impatiently. "Don't
you see? Everyone thinks I am the
informer, so they will be careful about
me. They hardly speak to me. But the real
informer can keep on passing along more
information to the police."

"Oh, Ivan! Tell Poppa! I'm scared."

Ivan paced restlessly to the window
and back, unable to keep his body still
while his mind was in an uproar. In less
than an hour, Momma would be home. Ivan
was thankful that there was that much
time before she was to arrive. He
glanced out at the street as if to assure

himself that she was not coming. What he saw drained the color out of his face.

"Katya!" His heart was pounding. "Sit down and pretend to do your homework."

Katya's eyes widened nervously.

"The police who questioned me last Sunday are turning into our building."

Katya gasped.

"They may not be coming here. Katya, you must not look afraid."

There was a loud pounding on the door.

The two officers looked exactly as they had before. Their eyes swept the small apartment as they entered. No, it did not matter that the parents were not yet home from work. It was Ivan to whom they wished to speak. It would be convenient, perhaps, for little sister to wait in another room? This did not concern her.

Ivan admired Katya's dignity as she picked up her notes and went into the bedroom, closing the door behind her with a respectful smile at the police. He could imagine how she would be sitting, trembling, on the bed. He knew she was praying.

As the police talked, Ivan was astonished that they knew he was suspected by his friends of being an informer. And they had been at school checking his grades. How Sophia Kutskova would have assured them she was doing everything she could to draw Ivan away from the superstition of his parents!

Comrade Lutsgov's voice remained friendly.

"I see from your school records you are following our great leader Lenin's advice when he said, 'Study, study, and study!' "

"Yes, comrade." Ivan felt uncomfortable.

"You do follow the teachings of Lenin, then?"

"Some of them. You know I am a Christian." Lenin, like Marx, had said, "Religion is the opiate of the people."

The short officer sighed impatiently. "We do not think this childish faith of yours will last long. We have already written down your name in a police file. Think of it, young comrade. You are just a boy, and yet your name is with those who resist the glorious new world our leader Lenin called us to."

Comrade Yakov put an arm around Ivan's shoulders. Ivan tried not to stiffen. "It is not too late for you, Ivan Nazaroff. We need intelligent boys like you to serve

Mother Russia. We can see to it, Ivan, that you can play hockey on any Soviet teams you're good enough for." Ivan's heart lurched. "But I think it is history, also, that you love. We can give you entrance to Moscow University, in years to come, if you will put aside this foolish Christian fable and help us. You could become a great historian someday."

Ivan was torn between wishing his mother would come home and fearing that the door would open and she *would* be there.

"Don't you want to continue your education?"

Ivan swallowed. "Yes, comrade. With all my heart."

"But you know very well it will be almost impossible for you to go to university if you are not a member of the Young Communist League."

"But I cannot join." Ivan hoped he sounded respectful.

"Of course you can." Yakov drew him to the sofa, and together they sat down. The short officer stood by the window, watching the street.

"That is why we are here. You can stay within your group of believers. Go to little meetings like last Sunday's, as before. From time to time, answer some questions for us about the other believers. You will not have to join the Communist party openly. You will nobly serve our glorious motherland. Ivan, already your 'Christian' friends have turned against you."

The second officer turned from the window, smiling. "We can see to it that they no longer will believe that you are the informer. It would be necessary to remove that impression!"

"How could you do that?"

"How?" The officer chuckled good naturedly. "By letting it leak out who the real informer is. These things are easily arranged."

It would be a truly wonderful thing, Ivan thought, no longer to be suspected. And for the real informer to be found out! The whole church would be safer then.

Comrade Yakov sighed. "If we were not concerned for you, Ivan Nazaroff, if we did not care about your future, why would we come here? You are our young comrade. A great future can be yours. We are extending to you the hand of brotherhood. Join us!"

◆Ambush

They had given him a week to decide. Ivan tossed on his bed night after night, his mind a storm of thoughts. Perhaps he could pretend to cooperate with the police. Then the real informer would be exposed as they promised. It might be that he could give worthless information to the police. But could he? They would find out. What would happen to him then?

Walking to school, Ivan imagined his coming meeting with the police. If he refused, what would they do? A cold fear swept over him.

And how would he ever become free from the label of *informer?* One of the other boys was guilty, perhaps every day giving information to the police without any fear of suspicion. Ivan couldn't imagine any of his friends doing such a thing. But it had been done!

Ivan had been glad for the thick door between the living room and bedroom. If Katya had heard the police asking him to inform, she would have immediately told their parents when they returned from work. As it was, he had enough trouble persuading her that nothing would be gained by worrying Momma and Poppa about a second questioning.

It was a Christian shortwave program that gave Ivan direction. The radio preacher had been talking about a man, Daniel, who was sentenced to death in a den of many hungry lions. Daniel had refused to obey the wrong laws of his government.

But God had not let Daniel be harmed. By a miracle, he had closed the jaws of the lions, and Daniel had not been eaten. Ivan listened closely.

"I am innocent before God," Daniel had declared to his king. That was why he had been safe from the lions. God had protected him.

Would God protect me from the anger of the police if I refuse to inform? Ivan wondered to himself. The radio pastor continued with his sermon, but Ivan was left behind in his thoughts. Quietly a *yes* seemed to grow within him. God *would* protect him! His spirit lifted in a freedom he had not felt for a long time.

But God had not spoken to him about Sophia Kutskova, Ivan thought grimly, as he recopied a history chart for his teacher. Nothing he could do these days seemed to satisfy her. She had not mentioned to him that the police had asked her questions about Ivan. But her impatience with him seemed to grow day by day. She began to make teasing remarks to the class about Ivan's Christianity. She had never done this before.

Today she was angry. Why could Ivan not understand the most simple directions? Perhaps all the religion he had collected into his head was festering there and making ordinary thought impossible. A ripple of laughter passed over the class. Ivan stared at his desk, his face red from embarrassment.

Later she stood next to his desk, speaking to the class in a grieved tone. "Ivan does not wish to represent our school in the all-Moscow history contest." Helpless, Ivan sat with his head lowered, desperately fighting back tears of disappointment and frustration at the news. "Perhaps, if he wanted, he could win for us. But such things do not interest him, I am afraid. It may be that he is too busy praying to God to work on such an earthly thing as a history essay for the honor of his school." Ivan could feel the disgusted glances of his classmates.

It was hard to have his hopes dashed so suddenly. He had been secretly dreaming that Sophia Kutskova would permit him to enter an essay in the contest, even if he were not a member of the Young Pioneers. There were no official rules against it. Of course, if he should win, his victory would be difficult for the Soviet public to understand. How could an uninformed Christian fanatic win a Russian history contest? But all the same, Ivan thought, she did not have to pretend to the class that he had refused.

But it seemed that all friendliness with his teacher was over. When her eyes met Ivan's gaze, she hardened her expression.

In the past, it had not been difficult to overlook the small spites of some of his classmates—his pencil deliberately broken if he left his seat or a foot stuck suddenly in the aisle as he walked to the chalkboard.

But today everything seemed to be going wrong. Vladimir Covich had given him a violent shove as the class stood for Sophia Kutskova's entrance into the room. Ivan had lurched forward, almost falling on his desk and hitting his side on its sharp corner. His muscles tensed with pain.

As the class seated itself, Vladimir had whispered, "Aren't you supposed to bless me, Christian?"

Later, as Ivan stood in turn to recite for his teacher, someone had quietly lifted his inkwell from its place on his desk and poured a thin trickle of ink across his notebook. Ivan was certain Sophia Kutskova had seen it happening. How could she not have seen? But she had said nothing. Ivan had to stay in the classroom during his lunch hour to recopy his ink-smeared work. His stomach growled with hunger.

By late afternoon, Ivan felt he was sick. He had a headache, and he could hardly force himself to do his work. He was afraid to raise his eyes from his desk and encounter the hard look of his teacher. His side ached.

Somehow it was Sophia Kutskova's

fault. Her taunting him these last few days had seemed to unleash in the class a spirit of hostility against Ivan that had never existed before. As the last bell rang, tears of relief sprang to his eyes. He was ashamed of how close to tears he had been all day.

There would be no waiting for Katya today. Ivan was going home, far away from school, as fast as he could. His heavy boots kicked a small spray of snow as he walked. Each step was that much farther from the school. Abruptly he stopped, his way blocked by Vladimir Covich and several other classmates.

"Ivan Nazaroff?" Someone behind him called his name commandingly. Swiftly Ivan turned his head, and immediately felt a sharp blow on his temple. A look of astonishment spread over his face, and then one of pain as he was hit hard in the stomach and on the jaw at the same time. Books flying, he skidded in the slippery snow and awkwardly tried to regain his balance.

"You need to learn a lesson, Nazaroff." There seemed to be a voice close to his ear. "You need to learn that we won't put up with you forever!" With the next

blow, Ivan was down in the snow. A warm trickle of blood caught in his eyelashes and smeared his cheeks. The boys were on top of him, delivering blow upon blow. Ivan felt as if he were suffocating with pain and fear. He coughed and cried and struggled against the weight of bodies and the flailing arms and fists. His head swam in blackness.

◆Discovery!

Pyotr's voice was coming from a long way off. He was calling insistently, but Ivan was too tired to answer. He wanted only to be left to sleep. But the calling continued. Ivan would have to answer. He was gathering strength to respond, when he realized Pyotr was not calling him. He was calling Fyodor. Gratefully, Ivan sank back into oblivion, only to be roused by a hand gently shaking his shoulder.

"Ivan! Ivan! Get up!" The voice had been calling him after all. He felt himself being pulled to his feet. Far-off pain made him open his eyes in bewilderment. The pain seemed to be spinning ever closer, like a hot meteor falling from the sky. Ivan groaned suddenly, as the meteor seemed to crash into his head.

"We'll help you, Ivan." Pyotr's voice was filled with concern. "Can you walk?"

Ivan tried to answer. His mouth felt huge and unworkable. Finally he groaned an assent, the pain pounding at him as if it wanted release.

"What is this? You have been fighting, Ivan?" Sophia Kutskova was out of breath, as if she had been running. "You have been fighting, Ivan?"

"Sophia Kutskova, we just now found Ivan in the snow."

"It looks as if he got the worst of the fight," the teacher replied coolly. "Such conduct is not permitted, as Ivan knows. Bring him to the principal." She turned and slowly led the way back into the school and along the first floor corridor to the principal's office.

"I can walk alone," Ivan gasped to Pyotr. "Tell Sophia Kutskova I don't need help." He was feeling better, except for the hammering in his head.

The principal invited him to sit down, and Ivan felt a surge of gratitude as he carefully lowered himself into the chair. Sophia Kutskova and the principal were talking quietly on the other side of the room. Finally the principal returned and looked sternly at Ivan. It was unfortunate that such a thing had occurred.

The principal regretted that any students at Moscow School Number 17 would choose such unpeaceful methods of settling disputes. He would not ask Ivan to report the names of the other boys. But clearly, Ivan had been fighting. He would have to be punished. A week's suspension from school was decided upon, and Ivan was directed to return home immediately. This incident, along with other things (the principal glanced sympathetically at Sophia Kutskova) would go on Ivan's record. The principal hoped that a week's absence from school would give Ivan time to think about his conduct and resolve to improve.

The bus ride home, with every movement of the vehicle shooting stabs of pain through Ivan's head and legs, the curious stares of people on the street—all seemed part of a dream to Ivan. Even the shock on his mother's face, the speed with which she eased him into bed, and the cool cloths on his head and hot towels on his aching legs seemed unreal.

There was something bothering Ivan, something that kept emerging from the pain in his head. It was not the beating. Such things had happened to others before,

and pain would go away. He remembered
Pyotr's voice coming from a long distance.
"Ivan! Ivan! Get up." That was not it.

In a rush, Ivan was in the schoolyard again, throwing snowballs at
Pyotr. Pyotr's eyes had been unfriendly
that day, too. It was Pyotr saying, "If you
are not the informer, Ivan, why would your
father be given his old job back?" It was
the look of sadness on Pyotr's face!

To Sophia Kutskova and his classmates,
Ivan was an outsider. Now, to his old
friends, Alexi, Fyodor, and Pyotr, he was an
outsider because they thought him to be
an informer. Loneliness far worse than
the pain swept over him. The informer had
to be found! He closed his eyes in a haze
of hurt.

It seemed only a moment later that
Momma was gently bathing his swollen
face in warm water. She was dressed for
work. Poppa had already left, and Katya
was hovering behind Momma, her eyes
rimmed with red. Ivan could not think why
Katya had been crying.

"Praise to the Lord," Momma was
saying, with a soft smile. "You slept all
night, Ivan. I'm sorry to wake you, but
Katya and I must leave soon."

A small tray with porridge and tea was on the table by his bed. Ivan tried to sit up. Pain in his shoulders and legs pushed him back against his pillow.

Katya gave a rueful smile. "To think the principal suspended you for a week, Ivan! As if you were not too injured to return!"

Momma was gently spooning porridge into Ivan's mouth. He shook his head and made another effort to lean on his arm. In his free hand he took the spoon and tried to swallow the cooled porridge. To please Momma, he drank some tea. She and Katya helped him to sit on the edge of the bed and finish the tea.

Ivan knew Momma wanted to stay home with him. But how could she explain such an absence at work? And Katya must go to school as usual. Enough attention had already been brought to the Nazaroff family.

The days at home passed very slowly. In the evenings, Ivan tried to respond cheerfully to the family's kind and affectionate attentions.

But at night, when the lights were out and Ivan lay restlessly on his bed, or during the long days when he was alone in the apartment, the problem of the informer's identity haunted him.

The answer came one evening as he was lying on the couch in the living room. His muscles were still sore and his head ached if he moved rapidly, but he had spent the day working on his schoolwork (or at least what he imagined his classmates might be doing) and had felt well. He had not spent time turning over and over in his mind the question of the informer. It was as if he had used up his quota of mental energy on that problem, and any attempt to return to it was met with a wall of mental rejection.

Their parents were visiting friends in the apartment building and Katya was pouring some tea she had made. Ivan sat up so suddenly he made Katya spill the tea.

"Katya! It just came to me! I know who the informer is!" Instead of protesting the spilled tea, Katya stared at him excitedly.

"Ivan! Who?" The pool of tea on the tray cloth was slowly growing larger and larger. For the moment, Katya was unconcerned.

"Katya! It's so simple! Listen!" Ivan swung his stiff legs off the couch and leaned toward his sister.

"First, Fyodor left Alexi's house and was picked up by the police. Later, I left, and they were waiting for me. Pyotr stayed for supper at Alexi's and then the police got him. They got Alexi last, after all had gone."

"I know all that!" Katya looked as if she would jump up and shake the information out of Ivan if he did not continue.

"But—" Ivan's voice lifted over his sister's, "when the police picked me up, they already had the paper with Scripture on it, and they knew that we had not simply been having a birthday party. They didn't bring the paper out until all the boys had been brought to the police station, but when they questioned me, they asked me if I knew what Jeremiah meant. They already had the paper before they questioned me!"

Katya's eyes were shocked. "That means Fyodor—"

"Yes! But *I'm* the only one who could know that for sure, because when you figure it out, the informer had to be either Fyodor or me, and it was not me!"

"You must tell Momma and Poppa."

Ivan felt a pang of regret at telling Katya. "No! It wouldn't do any good.

They don't know that my friends think I am an informer. Knowing would only worry them, and they would be as helpless as you or I in trying to take the blame off me."

Besides, something more was looming in Ivan's mind. In two days, he would have to return to the police station and give them his answer. This was a battle he had to fight alone.

◆In the lions' den

Perhaps he had made a mistake in not telling Katya he had to return to the police station. The crowd of students was thinning along the edges of the schoolyard, and a feeling of alarm came over Ivan. What if the police kept him for a long time? Katya was his link with home, and he was letting her slip away!

"Katya!" He could see her waiting in a long line at the bus stop. She turned her head, pleased that he was looking for her. His feet flew along the sidewalk, skillfully avoiding bumping into people as he ran. Fear that the bus would whisk her away gave speed to his still aching legs.

She made a place for him in the line. "It is so crowded today, you would think it was a holiday. Such long lines for the buses!"

Ivan was in a fever of impatience. "Katya! Listen. I have to go back to the police station for a little while."

His voice was low, but he could not resist a nervous glance over his shoulder. No one seemed to have heard.

Katya was frightened. "Ivan! What for? What has happened?"

"Nothing. Just listen. If I am late, you will know where I am. All right?" He turned swiftly.

"But wait, Ivan! Wait!" Katya could not leave her place in the long line to chase him for an answer. Gratefully, Ivan strode away. As he walked, he began to think about the radio sermon on Daniel in the lions' den.

It took him longer than he had expected to reach the police station. The streets were unusually full of people as he made his way through them, glad that he wasn't on the packed buses lurching by.

The iron gate of the police station clanged behind him with a grating sound that reminded Ivan uncomfortably of prison cells. But there was nothing to be nervous about. A simple matter. He had only to tell the police captain that he did not wish to be an informer. He had done nothing wrong. But all the same, his heart began pounding wildly as he approached the reception desk of the police station.

The officer was writing rapidly. A phone was ringing. People were coming and going at a fast pace. Ivan's eyes strayed to a guard at the head of a corridor, whose drab green uniform was almost gray in the shadow. Slung over his shoulder, his rifle glinted in the pale electric light.

Finally the comrade officer at the desk lifted his eyes to Ivan. He looked annoyed.

"What is it, young comrade? We are busy today."

At that moment, Comrade Yakov stepped out of a room into the dim corridor and hurried to the front desk with a sheaf of papers.

"I have an appointment with him—with Comrade Yakov." Ivan looked appealingly at the officer, waiting to be recognized.

Yakov groaned. "I have no time today."

Ivan's heart leaped with joy. So the Lord would shut up this lion's mouth! But the next moment his hopes fell just as suddenly, as the officer said, "Never mind. Come to my office. Ah! What a day!"

Yakov stood at his desk looking at Ivan. His voice was impatient.

"Now, Ivan Nazaroff, you have had a

week to think over my offer. Are you tired of your friends blaming you unjustly for being an informer? I would wish for them they could be of such a service to Mother Russia! Have you found out that the love that you believers talk about doesn't go very far?"

Ivan spoke carefully. "I think, comrade, that there *is* real love among Christians, even though it doesn't seem—"

"No! It *doesn't* 'seem'! But I am very busy this afternoon. Shall I simply assume, then, that an intelligent young man like you has decided to prove himself a good citizen, and as a result enjoy all the benefits of our glorious revolution?"

A car started suddenly in the street outside the window. Ivan paled. It had sounded, for a moment, like a lion's roar.

Taking a full breath, Ivan chose his words as carefully as possible.

"I am sorry, Comrade Officer. I cannot become an informer. And in truth, there would be nothing to tell you. Believers do nothing against the Soviet Union or against the laws of our country—"

Yakov growled in anger. A small nerve twitched in his cheek. "Ivan Nazaroff, I do not have time this afternoon for this kind

of talk. You have been given an unusual opportunity. Yet you spurn it. You were involved in an illegal meeting, yet no fine was placed upon your parents. We were willing to overlook what happened because of your age. Certainly we expect you to come to your senses—"

An officer in full uniform poked his head in the door and took in the scene. Comrade Yakov nodded as if in response to a command. The officer disappeared.

"You are making a very serious mistake." He paused, apparently more irritated than ever at Ivan's silence. "Today, of all days, I do not have time to discuss the fate of one stupid boy. Do you realize there has been a breakdown in our great Moscow subway system—something electrical—and the trains on one section have stopped? Transportation is critical. I am needed elsewhere. Yet you stand here and waste my time."

A phone was ringing in the distance. Ivan could hear hurried voices. Comrade Yakov looked furious for a second, then barked, "Go home!"

A joyful relief flooded Ivan.

"And go quickly, before I make you wait here all night."

His steps clicked rapidly down the corridor. Ivan stood for a second in the dim afternoon light. His hands were still clenched nervously at his side. A slow smile spread over his face, as with a sudden happy movement he wound his woolen scarf around his neck. He made his way, hands in pockets, past the reception desk and the officer at the desk, now almost hidden by a commotion of milling people.

Even in the lions' den! Ivan was exulting as he made his way through the ever more congested streets. *Even in the lions' den, the Lord kept me safe.*

Arriving home, Ivan at last could tell his parents all about the troubles and doubts he had gone through in the past few days. His words tumbled out joyously as he told how good God had been to him.

What could one do but celebrate, Momma and Poppa decided. It was a bad thing that Ivan had not told them about the police asking him to inform. This was too heavy a burden for a boy to bear alone. And going to the police station without telling them! What if something had happened?

Poppa kept shaking his head in pleasure

and praising God for the breakdown of the subway system.

"If the officer had not been so busy with the transportation problems, he might have kept you at the station for hours. Perhaps overnight. To think how the Lord protected you! To think how it was this day, and no other, that it happened that you had to go! Praises! Praises to God!"

Ivan felt almost as giddy as Katya, who was whirling about the apartment, perching for a moment on a chair or on the couch and leaping up, hugging Ivan until he insisted he had had the last hug he would endure.

Later, as the family sat around the large table in the living room drinking steaming glasses of tea and eating bread and butter and Momma's homemade jam, they began to piece together the events of the past few weeks.

Poppa spoke slowly with good humor.

"When I was reported at the factory, my records were studied. I think it was clear to the police that I had done nothing wrong and that the man who reported me was lying. But it was, after all, an opportunity to ask me questions and to show me that those who are Christians are not friends of the state."

Katya choked on her bread. "Even though you love our country and have served faithfully in the army!"

Poppa shook a finger at her, smiling gently. "Oh, that was very long ago, Katychka. That no longer counts."

Momma took the story up. "When you would not answer questions about the other believers, it was thought that perhaps your son could be made useful."

"Yes! The police thought that if they could make Ivan angry at being falsely accused of informing, he would give up his beliefs and even spy for them."

Ivan felt a rather unpleasant sensation in realizing he had been the center of police attention. "When the police discovered that I had been at a Bible study, they planned a way to encourage me to inform. By giving you back your old job at the factory, Poppa, it would look as if I *had* informed, and the others would be suspicious of me."

"Which is exactly what happened." Katya was biting with enthusiasm into her second piece of bread and jam.

Momma smiled proudly. "Except that

you did not agree to inform for them, Ivan."

"But there is something I do not understand." Poppa rubbed his head reflectively. "Why did the police *want* Ivan to become an informer? If Fyodor is an informer, as Ivan believes, there would be no need to have two to report on our group of believers."

The family fell silent. It was a good question. But then, the ways of the police were past finding out.

◆A new beginning

Now that the dreaded police interview was in the past, Ivan wanted to start life afresh. After an examination in school, one went the next day to a new section of material, perhaps a new textbook. At least one began a new page in one's notebook. It was satisfying to be able to put the old behind, and to begin anew. But life was not like that.

Unfortunately, Ivan was greatly behind in his work. The week of suspension had resulted in Ivan's missing a large amount of classwork. Sophia Kutskova offered him no help in getting caught up. She ignored his return and overlooked his raised hand in the question period following the lectures.

He wondered who had been chosen as the class candidate for the all-Moscow essay contest. Perhaps Sonya Sorina. She was very good in history, Ivan knew.

In spare moments during the day, Ivan thought about Fyodor betraying their small Bible study to the police. It was very difficult to believe such a thing of Fyodor. The boys and their families had been friends for many years. Every spring Fyodor's family had gone with Ivan's family to the Easter service in the forests outside Moscow. Ivan was remembering Fyodor slushing through the snowy mud, embarrassed by his too-large boots. How they had teased him!

His mother was a courageous woman. Once a week, in the evening after work, a small group of women gathered in her home under the pretense of an embroidery club. They would sit, needles flashing in the lamplight, singing hymns and sharing Bible verses and praying for one another.

It was difficult to believe Fyodor could have informed.

"Ivan Nazaroff?"

Ivan was trying to button his coat with one hand, holding his books in the other arm. He turned in surprise at the friendly tone. Sonya Sorina waited shyly, while the rest of the class streamed out of the room, happy to be gone.

"We get the same bus, Ivan. May I walk and talk with you?"

The crowded halls made talking impossible, and they walked together without trying to communicate until they were outside. Ivan glimpsed Alexi and Fyodor hurrying ahead of them. Fyodor cast a look over his shoulder at Ivan, then turned quickly back. Ivan was shocked at his face. Fyodor looked very tired. Perhaps sick.

Ivan's guess about Sonya had been correct. Sophia Kutskova had chosen her as the competition candidate. Sonya's red neck scarf had been caught in the collar of her coat when she put it on, and it seemed to point accusingly at Ivan.

She had been working on her essay, but she was concerned about it. It was against the contest rules for her to ask the advice of her teacher. But would Ivan read it? She smiled hopefully as she stepped up into the bus ahead of him.

"Of course, Sonya!" Ivan smiled back eagerly. "I am not sure that you need any help from me, but if you have your essay with you, I'll take it home and read it tonight." Ivan was enjoying talking to a classmate again.

Sonya glanced quickly at Ivan, then down at her gloved hands in her lap. "I'm sorry about what happened to you, Ivan. I mean the beating. It was cruel of the boys to do that, and you were very good not to tell on them. Many students in the class admire you for not telling and for not trying to pay them back."

Ivan stared at Sonya in surprise. Could it be true that he had friends in the class? His voice was low. "I thought that everyone was angry at me because I don't wear the red scarf and because I could not enter the contest."

Sonya shook her head. "Lenin himself said that there would be freedom of religion in Russia. I do not believe in any god, Ivan, but I know that it is not according to Lenin to be unjust to those who do. Others feel this way. You will see."

That evening, Momma brought out her embroidery and sat at the table with Ivan and Katya as they did their homework. Poppa was in his chair, listening to music on the radio and reading. It was a peaceful scene, and Ivan raced through page after page of homework, more industrious than he had been in a long time.

Momma's voice broke the silence. "I was at Fyodor's house last evening. It was our Bible study."

Katya's and Ivan's pens stopped in midsentence.

"I was telling the sisters about Ivan and how the police had tried to persuade him to be an informer. And how he had refused." Her eyes rested with a soft pride on Ivan's startled face. "Why should I not tell?"

"But Fyodor's *momma?* You talked to her about informers?" Ivan marveled.

"She does not know, Ivan, if Fyodor *did* inform on your Bible study at Alexi's. All the women rejoiced for you, Ivan, and so did I."

Momma bent her head over her sewing, and said no more.

In later years, Ivan was to remember the next morning as a shower of white. Snow was falling as he stood on the cold floor by his bed, and the window was white with frost, with only the top of the pane clear enough for him to see the huge swirling flakes outside.

Momma had a simple white cloth on the breakfast table, and Katya's fresh face above her thick white sweater smiled over the bread and tea. The winter light in the room was bright.

They had all been surprised at the early pounding on the door. Poppa had left for the factory, but Momma, who was getting ready to leave, pulled open the door in astonishment. Covered with a thick layer of light snow stood Alexi, Pyotr, and Fyodor, smiling shyly and asking to come in.

It was a few minutes before the boots were pulled off, the coats shaken in the hall, and the boys sitting at the table, glasses of amber tea warming their red fingers.

Katya sat dumbfounded at this unexpected visit, her eyes straying to Fyodor's face and moving away at the warning in her mother's eyes. There was laughing and what Katya called "warming up talk" and then a stillness fell over the group.

Fyodor cleared his throat. He was looking at Ivan. "I've come, Ivan, to tell you that I have done you a great wrong. I—I confessed this wrong to my family last night, and to the families of Pyotr Kachenko and Alexi Petrovich. They have forgiven me."

He shifted in his chair. "It was I who informed on the meeting at Alexi's. I permitted you to be blamed for it, and I was afraid to speak up. Although I didn't mean it, my silence led the police to try to make you an informer and caused you much suffering. I am asking a very great thing of you. I am asking you to forgive me."

Many times Ivan had seen his father embrace a Christian friend. It was the Russian way. They would fling their outstretched arms around each other, slapping each other's backs, their faces wreathed in smiles.

In a moment he was on his feet. Seeing the smile on his face, Fyodor stood uncertainly by his chair. In a huge embrace, Ivan threw his arms around his friend. Never had Ivan felt so much like a Russian.

"Thank you, Fyodor! Thank you for telling me. All is well now."

Fyodor tried to brush away the tears that were brimming in his eyes, as he continued.

"It was all an accident, from the very beginning. When I came out of Alexi's, the police picked me up. They knew about

Momma's Bible studies and wanted to ask me questions. I thought that somehow they had found out about *our* meeting and were questioning me about that. When I got to the police station, I was confused trying to answer about the birthday party. What made everything worse was that the paper, with the verses of Scripture on it, was in my pocket with my gloves. I must have put my gloves on top of the paper and then picked it up with them and put the paper and my gloves in my pocket together. To think of how we looked for it!"

Ivan began to laugh. Now that the problem was past, it all seemed amusing. Soon the boys and then Katya and Momma were laughing.

"When I was about to leave the police station, I took my gloves out of my pocket. Out fell the paper. The police read it and then made me take off my coat again. I had already told the names of those at the birthday party."

"As did I," Ivan assured him.

"So that is how it all came to be. After it happened, I was a coward not to tell the truth about it. But I made myself think it didn't matter. My parents will explain

everything to the believers, Ivan. No one will think of you as an informer again."

Alexi slapped Fyodor on the back. "Nor are you an informer, Fyodor! It was not intended."

"No! It was not." Fyodor looked so fierce, Katya thought she would laugh again. "They did try to make me agree to keep on bringing them information whenever I could, but I would not!"

"That's the part we couldn't understand," Ivan declared. "Why the police would want me to inform, when they already *had* an informer in our ranks." He looked shyly at Fyodor. "I knew it was you, Fyodor."

"I thought you suspected, Ivan. You knew the informer was not you, and it had to be one of us. I have been so ashamed."

Momma cleared away the glasses of tea as she spoke. "It is a good life we believers have! We can always make a new beginning."

"Yes! It is very good!" Ivan smiled in happiness at his three friends. In a few moments they were making their way to school through the snowy streets. The world was white.

> When thy people Israel be smitten down before the
> enemy, because they have sinned against thee. . . . If
> they sin against thee, (for there is no man that sinneth
> not,) and thou be angry with them, and deliver them to
> the enemy. . . .
>
> 1 Kings 8:33,46

All the people of Israel had to do to maintain the copious
blessings of the Lord was harken diligently to the Lord's
commandments, love the Lord, and serve Him with all their
hearts and souls. God promised blessings beyond anything
they could imagine. God promised them:

> There shall no man be able to stand before you: for the
> Lord your God shall lay the fear of you and the dread of
> you upon all the land that ye shall tread upon. . . .
>
> Deuteronomy 11:25

Israel was told, "Behold, I set before you this day a blessing
and a curse; A blessing, if ye obey. . . . And a curse, if ye . . .
turn aside out of the way . . ." (Deuteronomy 11:26–28).

Is This Generation Bringing a Curse on Itself?

Such a very clear manifestation of God at work must not be
lost on us today. Is this why we are falling, as victims, before
our modern enemies? We do not fight against flesh and blood
enemies; ours are more powerful! Our enemies are fear, depression, guilt, condemnation, worry, anxiety, loneliness,
emptiness, despair.

Has God changed in His character, or does He still stir up
adversaries against a sinning, compromising generation? Can
it be that these modern-day enemies are overpowering many
of God's people because of their hidden sins and backsliding?

It was not a heavy yoke God put on His people. It was so
simple and easy: Obey and be blessed, or disobey and suffer!

That same message is echoed in the New Testament: "For to be carnally minded is death; but to be spiritually minded is life and peace" (Romans 8:6).

We have had quite enough teaching on how to cope with our problems and fears. We have not had enough teaching on how to deal with sin in our lives. You can't heal cancer by putting patches on it. It has to be removed. We will continue to be a neurosis-bound people as long as we excuse the sin in us. No wonder we are so depressed, worried, and burdened with guilt and condemnation; we continue to live in our disobedience and compromise.

Most of us are fully aware sin is at the root of all our problems. We know sin causes fear, guilt, and depression. We know it robs us of all spiritual courage and vitality. But what we do not know is how to overcome the sin that so easily besets us.

Most of the books I've read about achieving Christ's righteousness and living a holy life never tell me how to get and keep the victory over sin. We hear it preached at us all the time: "Sin is your enemy. God hates your sin. Walk in the Spirit. Forsake your evil ways. Lay aside that sin you keep indulging in. Don't be bound by the cords of your own iniquity." That's all well and good.

You Can't Just Walk Away From Your Besetting Sin

How do you overcome a sin that has become a habit? Where is the victory over a besetting sin that almost becomes a part of your life? You can hate that sin; you can keep swearing you will never do it again; you can cry and weep over it; you can live in remorse over what it does to you; but how do you walk away from it? How do you reach the point where that sin no longer enslaves you?

Recently I asked over three hundred seekers a very pointed question: "How many of you are fighting a losing battle against a besetting sin? How many have one secret sin that keeps dragging you down?" I was shocked at the quick reaction. Almost all of them admitted they were victims, seeking desperately to be delivered from sins that bound them.

Everywhere I go, I hear such horrible admissions of defeat and failure concerning this matter of victory over a besetting sin. Most are dedicated Christians who deeply love the Lord. They are not wicked or vile people; it's just that they have to admit, "I have this *one* problem that keeps me from being totally free."

The confessions are honest and heartrending:

- I can't tell anybody what my secret battle is; it's between the Lord and me. I've prayed for deliverance for over three years now. I've made a thousand promises to quit. I've lived in torment. The fear of God haunts me. I know it's wrong. But, try as I may, I keep doing it. I sometimes think I'm hooked forever. Why doesn't the Lord come down and take this thing away?

- You tell me to lay aside my sin? Great! I've done that hundreds of times. But my sin won't let go of me. Just when I think I've gotten the victory—WHAM—it comes back again. I've cried a river of tears over my sinfulness, and I'm tired of promising God I'll never do it again. All I want is to be free, but I don't know how. I know I'll never be what God wants me to be until I get the victory.

- I've been preaching to others for over fifteen years, but recently I fell into Satan's trap. I've been crippled spiritually, and, as much as I hate my besetting sin, I can't seem to get free of this bondage. None of the formulas and solutions I preached to others seem to work for me. Frankly, I wonder how long God will put up with me before I'm exposed.

Is There Victory Over All Our Habitual Sins?

I have no formulas, no simple solutions. I do know there is much comfort in the Bible for those who are fighting battles between the flesh and the spirit. Paul fought the same kinds of battles, against the same kinds of enemies. He confessed, "For the good that I would I do not: but the evil which I would not, that I do" (Romans 7:19).

Paul cried out, just as all mankind does, "O wretched man that I am! who shall deliver me from the body of this death?" (Romans 7:24). He goes on to say, "I thank God through Jesus Christ our Lord . . ." (Romans 7:25).

Yes, we know. Victory over all our enemies is through Jesus Christ the Lord. But how do we get the power out of His vine into our puny little branches? How does this thing work? I love Jesus—always have. I know He has all power. I know He promises me victory, but just what does it mean? How does the victory come? It's not enough to be forgiven; I must be free from going back to my sin.

I am just beginning to see a little light on this great mystery of godliness. God is asking me to do the following three things in my own search for total victory over all my besetting sins:

1.   I must learn to hunger for holiness and to hate my beset-ting sin.   Every waking moment I must remind myself God hates my sin, mostly because of what it does to me. God hates it because it weakens me and makes me a coward; then I cannot be a vessel of honor to do His work on earth. If I excuse my sin as a weakness, if I make myself believe I am an exception and God will bend over backwards to comply with my needs, if I put out of mind all thoughts of divine retribution, then I am on the way to accepting my sin and opening myself to a reprobate mind. God wants me to loathe my sin, to hate it with all that is within me. There can be no victory or deliverance from sin until I am convinced God will not permit it!

The knowledge of God's retribution against sin is the basis of all freedom. God cannot look upon sin; He cannot condone it; He cannot make a single exception—so face it! It is wrong! Don't expect to be excused or to be given special privileges. God must act against all sin that threatens to destroy one of His children. It is wrong, and nothing will ever make it right! Sin pollutes the pure stream of holiness flowing through me. It must be confessed and forsaken. I must be convinced of that.

2. *I must be convinced God loves me in spite of my sin.* God hates my sin with a perfect hatred, while at the same time, He loves me with an infinite compassion. His love will never once compromise with sin, but He clings to His sinning child with one purpose in mind: to reclaim him.

His wrath against my sin is balanced by His great pity for me as His child. The moment He sees me hating my sin as He does, His pity conquers His loathing against sin. My motive must never be fear of God's wrath against my sin, but a willingness to accept His love that seeks to save me. If His love for me cannot save me, His wrath never will. It should be more than my sin that shames me and humbles me; it should be the knowledge that He keeps loving me in spite of all I've done to grieve Him.

Think of it! God pities me! He knows the agony of my battle. He is never far off; He is always there with me, reassuring me that nothing can ever separate me from His love. He knows my battle is enough burden, without forcing me to carry on with the added fear of wrath and judgment. I know His love for me will cause Him to withhold the rod while the battle is being fought. God will never hurt me, strike me, or abandon me while I am in the process of hating my sin and seeking help and deliverance. While I am swimming against the tide, He is always on shore, ready to throw me a lifeline.

3. *I must accept my Father's loving help in resisting and*

overcoming. Sin is like an octopus with many tentacles trying to crush out my life. Seldom do all tentacles loosen their hold on me at once. It is one tentacle at a time. In this war against sin, it is a victory won through one soldier dying at a time. Seldom does the entire enemy army fall dead at a single blast. It is hand-to-hand combat. It is one small victory at a time. But God doesn't send me out to do battle without a war plan. He is my Commander; I will fight—inch by inch, hour by hour—under His direction.

He dispatches the Holy Spirit to me, with clear directions on how to fight, when to run, where to strike next. This battle against principalities and powers is His war against the devil, not mine. I am just a soldier, fighting in His war. I may get weary, wounded, and discouraged, but I can keep on fighting when I know He must give me the orders. I am a volunteer in His war. I am ready to do His will at all costs. I will wait for His orders on how to win. Those directions come slowly at times. The battle seems to go against me, but in the end, I know we win. God wants me to just believe in Him. Like Abraham, my faith is counted to me as righteousness. The only part I can play in this war is to believe God will bring me, victorious, out of the battle.

Finally, When the Sin in Me Is Conquered, All My Other Enemies Must Flee

What I do about the sin in my life determines how my enemies will behave. Victory over besetting sin causes all my other enemies to flee. Worry, fear, guilt, anxiety, depression, restlessness, and loneliness are all my enemies. But they can harm me only when sin turns me into an unprotected target. The righteous are as bold as lions. They have clear minds and consciences, and those are fortresses these enemies cannot overrun.

Do you want victory over all your enemies? Then go at it the right way, by dealing ferociously with your besetting sin. Remove the accursed thing in your life, and you will become mighty in God. ". . . let us lay aside every weight, and the sin which doth so easily beset [surround or harass] us . . ." (Hebrews 12:1).

7

How to Win Over Temptation

Temptation is an invitation or an enticement to commit an immoral act. And right now Satan is raging over the earth, as a roaring lion, trying to devour Christians through powerful enticements toward immorality. No one is immune, and the closer you get to God, the more Satan will desire to sift you.

Sinners cannot be tempted; only true children of God can be. Rain cannot touch a body already under water. Sinners are already drowned in perdition. As children of Satan, they do as he dictates. They do not have to be tempted or enticed, because they are already immoral, already condemned. As slaves, they are not free to choose. They simply go from dead to twice dead to being plucked up by the roots. Sinners can be teased by the devil, but not tempted. Satan teases his own children into deeper and darker pits of immorality. They are already dead in their trespasses and sins and no longer fight the battles of the living. That's why our Lord tells us to rejoice when we fall into divers temptations. We are experiencing something unique only to maturing Christians.

Temptation is training under combat conditions. It is limited warfare. God limits that warfare to the point of being bearable. God wants combat-seasoned warriors who can testify, "I was under fire! I've been in the battle! The enemy was all around me, shooting at me, trying to kill me, but God showed me how to take it and not be afraid. I have experience now, so the next time I'll not fear."

Temptation is not a sign of weakness or a leaning toward the world. Rather, it is a graduation, a sign God trusts us. The Spirit led Jesus into the arena of temptation in the wilderness so He could learn the secret of power over all temptation. Actually God was saying to Jesus, "Son, I have given You the Spirit without measure. I have confirmed You before the world. Now I am going to permit Satan to throw at You every device he has, to tempt You with his most potent enticements. I will do this so You will never once fear his dominion, so You may go forth, preaching the kingdom, with faith that Satan is defeated; and You will know he cannot touch You in any way."

That is why Christians are tempted today—not to teach us something about ourselves, not to show off the power of the devil. No! Temptation is allowed in the saintliest of lives to teach us the limitation of Satan, to defang the devil, to expose his weakness, to reveal Satan as a scarecrow. We fear only what we do not understand.

Satan is just like the Wizard of Oz, who uses all kinds of scary devices to frighten unenlightened people. What a horror show he puts on: a tinseled display of power, strength, and dominion. But God knows it is all feeble noise and phoniness. Behind the stage is a weak wizard: the insignificant, powerless, bespectacled little bald-headed creature pushing buttons and pulling levers. Who in his right mind, knowing the mighty power of God, could but laugh at Satan's puny sideshow?

When we are tempted, it is God's way of saying to us, "Satan is powerless; he is not what he claims to be. He wears a false mask and shoots out fiery darts that fizzle and die in the presence of truth. But you must discover this yourself. Go into his circus. Stand up to his cheap threats, then conquer your fear of him. He will not scare you; he will not expose weakness in you. He cannot make you do anything. Instead, you will discover his weakness. You will expose him as a phony wizard. Then he will flee from you, because he doesn't want you to share with anyone else the secret you have learned."

It is not enough to say it is no sin to be tempted. That means absolutely nothing to those who have already yielded. The problem is not in learning how to accept temptation as an experience all Christians go through, but rather what to do to avoid giving in. The problem is how to bear up when Satan snares us in his trap! We want to know how to get the power and courage to say no and stick with it, how to find power to plan not to give in. When Satan comes in on us like a flood, there is no time to run to a secret closet for help. There may not be time to grab a Bible and seek out a few powerful promises to encourage us. There may not be a strong Christian friend around to hold us up in prayer. Suddenly temptation is upon us, and immediate decisions must be made. That makes it all the more important that Christians carry with them, at all times, the secret of bearing up anytime, anywhere, under any and all temptations.

Power to bear up and not yield to temptation does not come from stuffing our minds with Scripture verses, in making vows and promises, in spending hours in prayer and fasting, in surrounding ourselves with godly Christian friends and influences, or in giving ourselves over to a great spiritual cause. These things are all commendable and normal for Christian growth, but that is not where our victory lies.

Break the Fear of Satan's Power

The simple secret of bearing up under any temptation is to break the fear of Satan's power. Fear is the only power Satan has over man. God does not give us the spirit of fear; that is of Satan only. But man is afraid of the devil, demons, failure; that his appetites and habits can't be altered; that inner desires will erupt and control his life. He is afraid he is one of a thousand who may be different: innately weak, full of lust, and beyond help.

Man is afraid he can't quit his sin. He credits Satan with power he doesn't have. Man cries out, "I'm hooked! I can't stop. I'm spellbound and in the devil's power. The devil makes me do it!"

Fear has torment! As long as you are afraid of the devil, you can never break the power of any temptation. That is why Satan is promoting films like *The Exorcist, The Omen,* and a barrage of movies that make people vomit and faint in fear; that is why Satan is delighted with the teaching, now creeping into some churches, that demons can possess Christians. Satan thrives on fear, and Christians who are afraid of the devil have little or no power to resist his enticements.

It's all based on a lie! That lie is that Satan has power to break down Christians under pressure. Not so! Jesus came to destroy all the power of the devil over blood-washed children of God. I often wondered why God allowed spiritual people to be so tempted. Why doesn't God remove all temptation instead of "making a way of escape that we may be able to bear it"? (*See* 1 Corinthians 10:13.) The answer is simple: Once we learn how powerless Satan is, once we learn he can't make us do anything, once we learn God has all power to keep us from falling—then we can bear up under anything Satan throws at us. We can go through it without fearing we will fall!

The Move You Make Right After You Fail

You have heard it said it is not a sin to be tempted. I say it is not the greatest sin to give in to temptation. The greatest of all sins is not believing God has power to deliver us and keep us from yielding again! As a Christian, the most important move you will ever make is the move you make right after you fail!

We are not delivered from temptation, but from the fear of the devil to make us yield to it. We will keep on being tempted until we come to the place of rest in our faith. That rest is an unshakable confidence God has defeated Satan; Satan has no right or claim on us; and we will come forth as gold tried in the fire.

A double-minded person is unstable in all his ways. He is a person who believes the power is equally divided between God and Satan, which explains why some ". . . in time of temptation fall away" (Luke 8:13). They fall back into fear; they lose sight of God's mighty power; they cower under Satan's fear mongering. Jesus taught us to pray we not be led into temptation. We are to watch and pray that we "enter not into temptation." The spirit is willing, but the flesh is weak. The Spirit of God in us yearns to teach us confidence in God's power, but the flesh seeks to give in to fear.

I believe it was fear, not weariness, that put the disciples to sleep while Jesus prayed in the Garden. They had just received the news of His betrayal, that Jesus would be delivered into the hands of sinful men, that Peter would become a traitor, that they would all be offended and scattered. Suddenly they forgot all His miracles, His mighty power to heal the sick and raise the dead, His power to multiply loaves and fishes. They were now terrified. They feared for their flesh. They feared being abandoned by the Lord. They slept the sleep of doomed men.

When Jesus asks us to pray that we won't be led into temptation, He is actually saying, "Pray you learn to trust God's power now, instead of having to go back again and again into the arena of temptation, until the lesson is learned!" Pray you will not have to be led into temptation, because the lesson you would be taught has already been learned.

We Overcome by Faith Alone

The Bible says God knows ". . . how to deliver the godly out of temptations . . ." (2 Peter 2:9). How? By putting us under fire, until we come out singing, "Greater is he that is in me than he that is in the world" (*see* 1 John 4:4), until we learn we overcome by faith alone, until we acknowledge once and for all, ". . . For this purpose the Son of God was manifested, that he might destroy the works of the devil" (1 John 3:8).

You don't *have* to yield to temptation, but at times you may. Even the saintliest of God's people occasionally do. That is why God made special provisions for those who fail: ". . . if any man sin, we have an advocate with the Father, Jesus Christ the righteous" (1 John 2:1).

Our Lord is not nearly as grieved by our yielding to temptation as He is by our not learning how to deal with it. He is more hurt by the fact that we have not trusted His power to deliver. God is hurt, not so much by what we do, as He is by what we do not do. Jesus wept over the city of Jerusalem, deeply grieved; not because of the sin in that city; not because of the alcoholism, prostitution, adultery, lying, and cheating; but because He offered peace and deliverance, and they would not accept! They would not come in simple faith. They would not take Him at His word. They would not run to the shelter of His protecting wing. Their unbelief in His power made Him weep. A sinner is one who lives as one who confesses the devil has more power than God. The overcoming Christian is one whose life confesses, "God has the kingdom, the power, and the glory forever! Amen."

Some people really don't want to be free from their temptation. They flirt and play with it as a kind of spiritual brinkmanship. They know God can keep them from their sin, but deep inside they prefer to have a season of fun, a few rounds of immorality, a little taste of the forbidden. They are afraid to trust God for power to overcome, because they are not really sure they want out. It is too enticing! They don't want to grieve the Lord or turn their backs on His love. They want to be delivered—after a while. They want a halfway deliverance, just in time. Too many today are afraid to turn it all over to the Lord, because they still hunger after Satan's alluring enticement. Satan always makes yielding so convenient, so simple, so easy.

God Gives Us a Will to Overcome

God has the power to make us want to be free. He can put in us a will to overcome and the power to perform that will. If Satan can put a will in man to sin, God can and does put in His children the will to overcome. Our part is to simply believe God can sanctify our will and put in us an overpowering desire to resist the devil's invitation: "For it is God which worketh in you both to will and to do of his good pleasure" (Philippians 2:13).

Do you want power to bear up under all temptation? Do you want a way of escape? Do you want a growing strength to resist? Then quit glorifying the devil! Stop thinking he can force you to sin! He has no power to addict you to anything! Use your shield of faith! Look right into the eye of that storm of temptation, and cry out, ". . . that wicked one toucheth me not" (*see* 1 John 5:18). Conquer your fear of the devil's power, and you can forever after bear any temptation he sends your way. Simply commit the keeping of your faith unto Him, as a faithful Creator.

Most important of all remember this: ". . . stand fast. . . . And in nothing terrified by your adversaries . . ." (*see* Philippians 1:27, 28).

8

Christian, Lay Down Your Guilt

Christians are strange creatures. They travel the world, preaching the love of Jesus and His forgiveness for any and all sin. They tell the heathen, the addict, the alcoholic, the prostitute: "Come to Christ and be forgiven. He forgave your sins at the cross, so come and receive forgiveness and healing for all your hurts. You can have peace and be free of guilt." As a result, sinners who have been guilty of every conceivable kind of dark and evil deed gladly come to Christ and are instantly forgiven and delivered from their guilt.

The hardest thing in the world for the Christian to do is receive for himself the same kind of love and forgiveness he preaches to sinners. We Christians find it so very difficult to allow ourselves the same freedom from guilt we offer, through Christ, to harlots and drunkards.

Christians sin against the Lord, then proceed to carry about an excruciating load of guilt. They want to pay for their failure. They want to be punished. They want to do penance or suffer some kind of hurt before they are forgiven.

"But Lord," argues the Christian, "I sinned with my eyes wide open; I knew better. I knew before I did it I was breaking a commandment. How can I be forgiven for grieving my

Saviour by such insolence? I shook off the conviction of the
Holy Spirit and stubbornly went ahead and committed sin."

The Danger of Guilt

Guilt is dangerous in that it destroys faith. The enemy of
our souls is not at all interested in making Christians into
adulterers, addicts, or prostitutes. He is interested in one
thing only, and that is turning Christians into unbelievers. He
uses the lusts of the body to bind the mind.

Satan did not want Job to become an adulterer or an addict
to pain pills or a wine guzzler. No! Satan wanted one thing of
Job: He wanted him to curse God! He wanted to destroy Job's
faith in God.

So it is today. Our real battle is not really with sex, alcohol,
drugs, or lust. It is with our faith. Do we believe God is a
deliverer? Is He there to help in the hour of temptation? Are
His promises true? Is there freedom from sin? Is God really
answering prayer today? Will He bring us out of the battle,
victorious? Will joy follow weeping?

Satan wants you to be so crushed with guilt that you let go
of your faith. He wants you to doubt God's faithfulness. He
wants you to think nobody really cares, that you will live in
misery and heartbreak, that you will always be a slave to your
lust, that God's holiness is unreachable, that you are left alone
to work out your own problems, that God no longer cares
about your needs and feelings. If he can get you to the point of
despair, he can flood you with unbelief. Then he has suc-
ceeded in his mission. The three simple steps toward atheism
are guilt, doubt, and unbelief.

Guilt, like a raging cancer, can eat away at the spiritual
vitality of a Christian. It causes a person to lose control of life;
it leads to a desire to quit or retire from spiritual activity; and
it finally brings on physical pain and disease. Like cancer,

guilt feeds upon itself, until all spiritual life is gone. Weakness and a sense of shame and failure are the end results.

I meet Christians across this nation who go about continually burdened down by an overwhelming load of guilt. They have made themselves believe they are traitors to the Lord. They live in spiritual agony and grief every waking hour, because of some hidden sin or weakness. They cannot appropriate divine forgiveness for themselves, and they live in dreaded fear of God's judgment upon themselves or their families.

The Causes of Guilt

Who are these guilt-ridden, sad souls? It is often that married individual who, for years, has been a captive in a loveless marriage and finds someone else to light up his boring life. Somewhere along the way, that marriage lost its romance. Hurts would no longer heal; the lines of communication were cut. Then one day, without even seeking it, someone else enters the picture. A tender word, a tender touch, and there is a new kind of awakening. Someone else ignites those dying embers, and the secret love affair is born. They take comfort in the words of the song that says, "How can it be wrong, when it seems so right?"

Often there are children to consider, a reputation, a job, or a ministry. But the one thing above all else that brings on the guilt is the knowledge that God's laws are being broken. God won't smile on it; He won't put His blessing on it. Then the war begins. They are torn between a conviction of having finally found the one true love of life and the innate desire to stay true to God and marriage vows. And the guilt keeps piling up. They want out of a hopeless marriage, without displeasing God.

There are multiplied thousands caught in this kind of trap,

even ministers. The more they love God, the worse their guilt. A few are able to shake off the guilt and go about indulging their secret affairs, having justified their actions with elaborate excuses. But most cannot be dishonest with their· own hearts, so they go on living with accumulating guilt.

What about all those other secret lusts of the flesh which haunt the soul? What about the Christian who overindulges in drink on the sly or who has too many prescription drugs which have caused a dependency? What about the thousands of Christian men caught up in porno binges? A strange attraction sends them back into the X-rated movie houses or to the newsstands for nudie magazines—not once or twice, but nearly every time they are alone, especially when traveling. Yes, I'm talking about Christians.

Secret affairs, drinking, prescription drugs, pornography, homosexuality, lesbianism, and many other human weaknesses are all prime causes of guilt. The sinner can indulge in any or all of these sins and not battle with guilt, but not so for the true child of God.

Saints That Ain't

Sadly, many pious Christians hide behind puritan masks and go about like the publican of Christ's time, who boasted, "Thank God I'm not like such sinners." To hear them tell it, their marriages are flawless and their morals are saintlike. Don't believe it! We have all sinned and come short of God's holiness. There are none righteous in their own strength. Show me the saintliest soul on earth, and I'll show you one who battles temptation as much as any other Christian alive. And if a Christian would like to cure himself of being judgmental, all he has to do is look inside himself and be honest about his own inner struggles. That should keep us all from worrying about another's spiritual condition.

One of the good things that should come out of a Christian's inner struggle with the flesh is that he learns to quit throwing stones—that is, if he is honest with himself. The Word instructs, ". . . even as Christ forgave you, so also do ye" (Colossians 3:13).

Perhaps out of all the terrible struggles Christians are now enduring, we will discover a new spirit of tolerance and love for others. Perhaps, being forgiven so much ourselves, we will in turn forgive others, for their shortcomings: ". . . be ye kind one to another, tenderhearted, forgiving one another, even as God for Christ's sake hath forgiven you" (Ephesians 4:32).

Tested by the Word

Is there freedom from guilt? Can Christians deal with infatuations, addictions, and weaknesses in an honest and godly way and find true freedom from sin's power? Will God keep forgiving while the struggle goes on? If that besetting sin keeps overcoming the believer, will God continue to forgive until the victory comes?

There have been some very godly people who have confessed to me that God's Word tried them severely. The promises sound as if they should work almost automatically, but they don't. The commandment says don't, but our weak flesh can't seem to obey. We go ahead and do what we know to be sinful. The Word says, ". . . sin hath no more dominion over you" (*see* Romans 6:9). Yet it doesn't seem to work in everyday life.

> O wretched man that I am! who shall deliver me from
> the body of this death? I thank God through Jesus Christ
> our Lord. So then with the mind I myself serve the law
> of God; but with the flesh the law of sin.
>
> Romans 7:24, 25

The question is: Where do I get the power to resist the lust

of my heart? Is it sheer willpower? Do I grit my teeth and say,
"I'll simply walk away from it, never to let it hold me in its
power"? Does God expect me to resist with what I have? Can
I win over my besetting sin, in one moment of finality?

Others say glibly, "Just stop it! Quit it! Walk away from it!
You know better, so what's so difficult?" Oh, yes! But those
same people who find it so easy to walk away from all the lusts
of the flesh and the desires of the world find it nearly impossible to walk away from their own loneliness, sorrows, fears, or
struggles with health. Every Christian on this earth fights
inner battles; not one is immune!

The way to get rid of guilt is to get rid of sin. It sounds
simple, but it isn't. You don't just make up your mind to drop
the third party who has entered your life. Many have tried
that and found it didn't work. You don't just walk away from
things that bind. The Scripture haunts you; it says, "Put off
the old man. . . . Lay aside the besetting sin. . . . Flee the
appearance of evil. . . . Walk in the Spirit and you will not
fulfill the lusts of the flesh." That is exactly what you want:
freedom from the sin that so easily besets you, to walk in the
Spirit completely, and to live a life totally pleasing to God.
But you seem helpless in putting off those desires.

When you can't seem to overcome, and you keep falling flat
on your face, failure after failure, then you begin to think,
"Something is terribly wrong with me. I am a sensuous,
wicked, weak child. God must be fed up with all my failures.
I've made Him mad." That is when guilt floods in like a tidal
wave.

We All Face the Same Struggles

Take heart, child of God. Everybody is in the same boat.
Not all of us battle a secret affair or an addiction to the flesh.
Some of us struggle with a more insidious enemy: doubt. To
doubt God's concern and daily involvement in our lives can
cause terrible guilt. But there is no temptation befallen you

that is not common to all men. You are not going through some strange trial, unique only to you. Thousands more are going through the very same struggle.

The most important move you will ever make in your life is the move you make right after you fail God. Will you believe the accuser's lies and give up in despair, or will you allow yourself to receive the forgiving flow of God's love, which you preach so much to others?

Do you fear asking His forgiveness because you are not really sure you want to be free from that thing which holds you? Do you want the Lord, yet secretly long for something or someone not lawfully yours? God is able, in answer to sincere prayer, to make you want to do His perfect will. Ask Him to make you want to fulfill His will. "For it is God which worketh in you both to will and to do of his good pleasure" (Philippians 2:13).

When a Christian sins, he feels shut out of God's presence, just as Adam did. God is always there, waiting to talk, but sin causes man to withdraw. God never withdraws; only man withdraws. Actually the person living in sin is afraid to open up to God, for fear He will ask a commitment to holiness before the sin is ready to be surrendered. The sinning Christian knows this: "If I get close to Jesus, the Holy Spirit will put His finger on my secret sin, and I'll have to give it up. I'm not ready for that yet!"

It does no good to ask yourself, "How did I get into this mess? Why do I have to be tempted along these lines? Why such a trial, when I didn't ask for it or want it? Why me, Lord?" Don't blame the devil either. We sin when we are drawn away and enticed by the lust of our own hearts.

Don't Justify Your Weaknesses

Never justify your wrongdoing. There is only one way to become hardened by sin, and that is to justify it. Christians who learn to hate their sin will never give themselves over to its power. As Christians, we must never lose sight of the exceeding sinfulness of sin. Stay uncomfortable with your sin.

I heard it said of an evangelist who lives in open, shameless adultery, "Well, at least he is honest about it. He's not trying to hide his adultery, as some ministers, who do it on the sly." I see nothing honest in that at all! That adulterous evangelist has been totally blinded by a multiplicity of justifications. He has no guilt, because he has given himself over to a lie and has become the victim of a reprobate mind. On the other hand, the person who continues to struggle, hating a garment spotted, despising all sin against God, has all heaven standing by to help. Until the victory comes, continue to despise all your wrongdoing.

Never Limit God's Forgiveness

My dear Christian friend, never limit God's forgiveness to you. His forgiveness and longsuffering have no limit. Jesus told His disciples: "And if he trespass against thee seven times in a day, and seven times in a day turn again to thee, saying, I repent; thou shalt forgive him" (Luke 17:4).

Can you believe such a thing? Seven times a day this person willfully sins before my very eyes, then says, "I'm sorry." And I am to forgive him, continuously. How much more will our heavenly Father forgive His children who come in repentance to Him? Don't stop to reason it out. Don't ask how or why He forgives so freely. Simply accept it.

Jesus did not say, "Forgive your brother once or twice, then tell him to go and sin no more. Tell him if he ever does it again, he will be cut off. Tell him he is a habitual, hopeless sinner." No! Jesus called for unlimited, no-strings-attached forgiveness!

It is God's nature to forgive. David said, "For thou, Lord,

art good, and ready to forgive; and plenteous in mercy unto all them that call upon thee" (Psalms 86:5).

God is waiting, right now, to flood your being with the joy of forgiveness. You need only to open up all the doors and windows of your soul and allow His Spirit to flood you with forgiveness.

John, speaking as a Christian, wrote: "And he is the propitiation for our sins: and not for our's only, but also for the sins of the whole world" (1 John 2:2).

According to John, the goal of every Christian is to sin not. That means the Christian is not bent toward sin but, instead, leans toward God. But what happens when that God-leaning child sins?

> . . . And if any man sin, we have an advocate with the Father, Jesus Christ the righteous: If we confess our sins, he is faithful and just to forgive us our sins, and to cleanse us from all unrighteousness.
>
> 1 John 2:1, 1:9

Lay Down Your Guilt, Now

You don't just lay down your guilt, your sin, or your inner struggle as if it were a jacket you strip from your back. You lay it all down through a supernatural operation of God's Holy Spirit. The Holy Spirit responds to the broken heart that reaches out, in faith, to lay hold of God's promises. He then imparts His divine nature to that empty vessel. A miraculous series of events begins to unfold. Suddenly there comes to the saint of God a renewed desire to confess, to yield to God's will, to become more like Jesus, to see things in the light of eternity, to experience a rush of surrender.

The Holy Spirit brings the yielded vessel around to God's way of thinking. We go after things we believe are good for us; we covet what is not ours. But God looks way down the road, and He knows what is best. Our ways and thoughts are not His ways or His thoughts. God will give His surrendered child something even better, if he lays down his own plan.

What is it that stands between you and God? Is it a secret sin? Lust? Doubt? Fear? Anxiety? What is the cause of your guilt? Be willing to lay it down in surrender at the foot of the cross. Have a funeral right there; do your hurting and dying; then rise up in obedience, and walk in the Spirit. God will not let you down. He will replace that empty place with something far better, something pleasing to His own heart, something providing more joy to you than what you gave up.

Lay down your guilt, my friend. You don't need to carry that load another minute. Open up all the doors and windows of your heart, and let God's love in. He forgives you over and over again. He will give you the power to see your struggle through to victory. If you ask, if you repent—you are forgiven! Accept it now.

9

Stop Condemning Yourself

I feel so ashamed of myself when I think back over my early ministry, because I condemned so many sincere people. I meant well, and often my zeal was honest and well-meaning. But how many people I brought under terrible condemnation because they didn't conform to my ideas of holiness!

Years ago I preached against makeup on ladies. I preached against short dresses. I condemned everything that was not on my "legitimate" list. I have preached some very powerful sermons in the past, condemning homosexuals, divorcées, drinkers, and compromisers. I am still deeply committed to the idea that ministers must cry out against the inroads of sin and compromise in the lives of Christians. I still don't like to see Christian women painted up like streetwalkers. I still don't like mini-dresses. I believe, more than ever, that God hates divorce. I am still committed to the idea that God will not wink at any sin or compromise of any kind.

But lately God has been urging me to quit condemning people who have failed and, instead, preach to them a message of love and reconciliation. Why? Because the church today is filled with Christians who are burdened down with mountains of guilt and condemnation. They don't need more preaching about judgment and fear; they are already filled with enough fear and anxiety. They don't need to hear a preacher tell them how mad God is with them; they are already too much afraid of God's wrath. They need to hear the message John preached: "For God sent not his Son into the world to condemn the world; but that the world through him might be saved" (John 3:17).

Jesus said to an adulterous woman, ". . . Neither do I condemn thee; go, and sin no more!" (John 8:11). Now why can't I, and all my fellow ministers, preach that same kind of loving message to the multiplied thousands who live in fear and adultery? Why do we still condemn divorced Christians who remarry, when they have truly repented and have determined to sin no more in that manner?

Recently a ten-year-old lad stopped me after a crusade and begged me to hear his story. He was hysterical. "My mom and dad got divorced two years ago. Mom is a good Christian, and she married a nice Christian man. I live with mom and my stepdad, and I love them a whole lot. But my mom is always sad, and she cries a lot, because a minister told her she was living in sin. Is my mom going to hell because she got divorced and remarried another divorced man? I'm all confused, because they're both such good Christians."

I told that boy what I want to tell the whole world. If she divorced because of her own adultery and remarried, she is living in adultery. God hates adultery. But if she has repented, God forgives her, and she starts all over, like a newborn Christian. She is not living in sin when it is under the blood of Christ and forgiven. She can begin a new life without guilt or condemnation. If Jesus forgives murder, thievery, lying, and so on, He also forgives adultery.

It amazes me that we ministers are so willing to go to Africa to preach forgiveness to the heathen, but so unwilling to preach forgiveness and reconciliation to Christians at home. One minister complained to me about all the divorced, broken, troubled people in his new assignment. I thought, *My brother, you ought to be thankful God put you in such a fertile field. Those are the people who need your help the most. They need a man of God to show them how to begin anew.*

I am a happily married man; and, God helping me, Gwen and I will always be together, till death do us part. I despise divorce with a passion! But it troubles me that the church is willing to write off all those who have made a mistake. The church offers comfort and solace to all those who are the innocent victims—the wife who was cheated on, the husband whose wife walked out on him, all the children hurt in the separations.

But what about all the perpetrators—the sinners, the ones who wronged innocent loved ones? If one out of every three marriages ends in divorce, that means millions of husbands and wives are the guilty parties. I'm not willing to give up, even on the guilty ones. The thief Christ forgave at Calvary was not an innocent victim. No! He was a perpetrator; he was the criminal! But in his sin he turned to Christ in faith. He was forgiven and taken with Christ to glory.

What about homosexuals and lesbians and alcoholics? Will condemning them accomplish any good? No! A thousand times, no! Christ did not come to condemn these sinners, but to rescue them in love. God hates homosexual acts, but He does not despise people who do not live up to masculine or feminine roles.

A lovely nineteen-year-old nurse stopped me after a crusade. Tearfully, she sobbed out a pitiful confession: "Mr. Wilkerson, I'm a lesbian. I feel so dirty, so unclean. The minister of the church I used to attend asked me to never return. He said he couldn't take a chance on my seducing others in his congregation. I feel as if suicide is my only way out. I live in total fear and condemnation. Must I kill myself to find peace?"

She kept backing away from me, as if she were too unclean to be in my presence. I asked her if she still loved Jesus. "Oh, yes," she replied. "Every waking hour my heart cries out to Him. I love Christ with everything in me, but I'm bound by this terrible habit."

How beautiful it was to see her face light up when I told her how much God loved her, even in her struggles. I told her, "Don't ever give yourself over to your sin. God draws a line right where you are. Any momentum toward Him is accounted as righteousness. Any move back across that line, away from Him, is sin. If we draw near to Him, He draws near to us. Keep your spiritual momentum! Keep loving Jesus, even though you still do not have total victory. Accept His daily forgiveness. Live one day at a time. Be convinced that Jesus loves sinners, so He must love you, too!"

She smiled a smile of relief and said, "Mr. Wilkerson, you are the first minister who ever offered me a ray of hope. Deep in my heart I know He still loves me, and I know He will give me deliverance from this bondage. But I have been so condemned by everybody. Thanks for your message of hope and love."

Are you living under condemnation? Have you sinned against the Lord? Have you grieved the Holy Spirit in your life? Are you waging a losing battle with an overpowering temptation?

All you need to do is search God's Word, and you will discover a God of mercy, love, and endless compassion. David said: "If thou, Lord, shouldest mark iniquities, O Lord, who shall stand? But there is forgiveness with thee, that thou mayest be feared" (Psalms 130:3, 4).

A distraught woman who had come to my office sobbed, "Mr. Wilkerson, once God cured me of alcoholism. But recently I got discouraged and went back to drink. Now I can't stop. I've failed the Lord so badly that all I can do is give up. After all He did for me, look how I've failed Him. It's no use; I'll just never make it."

I'm convinced there are more spiritual failures than many of us realize. There is a demonic strategy to build such failures into walls to keep the defeated ones far from God. But we don't need to let the devil turn our temporary defeats into a permanent hell.

I believe there are literally millions of people like the young sailor who came to see me. With tears in his eyes he said, "My dad is a minister, but I've failed him so terribly. I'm so weak. I'm afraid I'll never serve the Lord as I should. I'm so easily led into sin."

Confessions such as these are tragic, but I have found great encouragement in the realization that some of the greatest men and women of the Bible had times of failure and defeat.

Would you consider Moses a failure? Hardly! He was to Israel what Washington and Lincoln, together, were to America—and much more. But look closely at the great lawgiver's life. His career began with a murder, followed by forty years of hiding from justice.

Moses was a man of fear and unbelief. When God called him to lead the Israelites out of slavery, he pleaded, ". . . I am not eloquent . . . I am slow of speech. . . . Send . . . by the hand of him whom thou wilt send" (Exodus 4:10, 13). This angered God. All his life, Moses longed to enter the Promised Land, but his failures kept him out. Even so, God compares Moses' faithfulness to Christ's. His failures did not keep Moses out of God's hall of champions: ". . . consider . . . Christ Jesus; Who was faithful to him that appointed him, as also Moses was faithful in all his house" (Hebrews 3:1, 2).

We usually think of Jacob as the great prayer warrior who wrestled with the angel of the Lord and prevailed. Jacob was given a vision of heaven with angels ascending and descending. Yet this man's life was filled with glaring failures, and Scripture does not hide any of them.

As a youth, Jacob deceived his blind father, to steal his brother's inheritance. Married, he despised his wife Leah, while he nursed a great secret love for her sister, Rachel. He did not accept his responsibility as a husband. After the birth of each man-child, Leah kept saying, ". . . Now this time will my husband be jointed unto me . . ." (Genesis 29:34). But the fact was that Jacob hated her.

Here was a man caught in a web of trickery, graft, theft, unfaithfulness, and polygamy. Nevertheless, we still worship the God of Abraham, Isaac, and Jacob.

King David, singer of Psalms and mighty warrior, delighted in the law of the Lord and posed as the righteous man who would not stand among sinners. Yet how shocking are the weaknesses of this great man. Taking Bathsheba from her husband Uriah, he sent that unsuspecting man to his death, at the front lines of his army. The Prophet Nathan declared that this double sin gave great occasion for the enemies of the Lord to blaspheme.

Picture the great king standing by the casket of his dead, illegitimate child, a stolen wife at his side, and a world filled with enemies who cursed God because of his notorious sins. David stood there, a total failure. Yet God called David a man after His own heart. He blessed the murderer Moses and the schemer Jacob, too, because these men learned how to profit from their failures and go on to victory.

If you are discouraged by your failures, I have good news for you. No one is closer to the kingdom of God than the man or woman or young person who can look defeat in the eye, learn to face it, and move on to a life of peace and victory.

Don't Be Afraid of Failure

This seems like an automatic reaction. When Adam sinned, he tried to hide from God. When Peter denied Christ, he was afraid to face Him. When Jonah refused to preach to Nineveh, his fear drove him into the ocean, to flee the presence of the Lord.

But God has shown me a truth that has helped me many times: Something much worse than failure is the fear that goes with it. Adam, Jonah, and Peter ran away from God, not because they lost their love for Him, but because they were afraid He was too angry with them to understand. Satan uses such fear to make people think there is no use trying.

That old accuser of the brethren waits, like a vulture, for you to fail in some way. Then he uses every lie in hell to make you give up, to convince you God is too holy or you are too sinful to come back. Or he makes you afraid you are not perfect enough or that you will never rise above your failure.

It took forty years to get the fear out of Moses and to make him usable in God's program. Meanwhile God's plan of deliverance had to be delayed for nearly half a century while one man learned to face his failure. If Moses or Jacob or David had resigned himself to failure, we might never again have heard of these men. Yet Moses rose up again to become one of God's greatest heroes. Jacob faced his sins, was reunited with the brother he had cheated, and reached new heights of victory. David ran into the house of God, laid hold of the horns of the altar, found forgiveness and peace, and returned to his finest hour. Jonah retraced his steps, did what he had refused at first to do, and brought a whole city-state to repentance and deliverance. Peter rose out of the ashes of denial to lead a church to Pentecost.

Despite Failure, Keep Moving On

It is always after a failure that a man does his greatest work for God.

Twenty-one years ago, I sat in my little car, weeping; I was a terrible failure, I thought. I had been unceremoniously dumped from a courtroom after I thought I was led by God to witness to seven teenage murderers. I had seen my picture in the tabloids, over the caption, "Bible waving preacher interrupts murder trial." My attempt to obey God and to help those young hoodlums looked as though it were ending in horrible failure.

I shudder to think of how much blessing I would have missed if I had given up in that dark hour. How glad I am today that God taught me to face my failure and go on to His next step for me.

I know of two outstanding men of God, both of whom had ministered to thousands of people, who fell into the sin David committed with Bathsheba. One minister decided he could not go on. Today he drinks and curses the Christ he once preached about. The other man repented and started all over. He now heads an international missions program which reaches thousands for Christ. His failure has been left behind. He keeps moving forward.

In my work with narcotics addicts and incorrigibles, I have observed that the majority of those who return to their old habits become stronger than all the others when they face their failures and return to the Lord. They have a special awareness of the power of Satan, a total rejection of confidence in the flesh.

Despite Failure, Continue to Worship

There was only one way for Moses to stay in victory, because he had a disposition like so many of us today. He continually communed with the Lord, ". . . face to face, as a man speaketh unto his friend . . ." (Exodus 33:11). Moses maintained that close friendship with God. I believe the secret of holiness is very simple: Stay close to Jesus! Keep looking into His face, until you become like the image you behold.

One evening, a hysterical woman stopped me on the street and blurted out a terrible confession. Clutching my sleeve so hard I thought she would tear it, she said, "Mr. Wilkerson, I am facing the darkest hour of my life. I don't know which way to turn. My husband has left me, and it's all my fault. When I think of how I failed God and my family, it is almost impossible for me to sleep at night. What in the world am I going to do?"

I was moved to tell her, "My friend, lift up your hands, right now on this street corner, and begin to worship the Lord. Tell Him you know you are a failure, but you still love Him. Then go home and get on your knees. Don't ask God for a thing, just lift your heart and your hands and worship Him."

I left that lady standing on the street corner, with her hands raised to heaven, tears rolling down her cheeks, praising the Lord and already tasting the victory that was beginning to surge back into her life.

Now let me talk about your failure. Is there trouble in your home? Has some despised habit gripped your life so hard you can't seem to break it? Are you tormented in mind or spirit? Has God told you to do something you have failed to do? Are you out of the will of God? Are you hounded by memories of what you were at one time or by visions of what you can be? Then worship the Lord in the midst of your failure! Praise Him! Exalt Him!

All this may sound like an oversimplification, but the way past failure is simple enough for children, fools, and Ph.D.'s to follow successfully. Christ says: ". . . him that cometh to me I will in no wise cast out" (John 6:37). "Come unto me, all ye [failures] that labour and are heavy laden, and I will give you rest" (Matthew 11:28).

Don't be afraid of failure. Keep going on in spite of it. Worship God until victory comes.

The hardest part of faith is the last half hour. Keep going, and you will yet face your finest hour.

10

When You Don't Know What to Do

What would you think if our president, addressing the nation on network TV, confessed, "We really don't know what to do. Your leaders are confused, and we have no sense of direction." That would be some kind of speech. The nation would be convulsed with ridicule and scorn for him and all his associates.

That is exactly what King Jehoshaphat did. Three enemy armies were closing in on Judah, and this mighty leader called the nation together at Jerusalem to formulate a war plan. He needed plans, a decisive declaration of action. Something had to be done immediately. Instead, Jehoshaphat stood before his people and poured his heart out to God in confession:

> Behold, I say, how they reward us, to come to cast us out of thy possession, which thou hast given us to inherit. O our God, wilt thou not judge them? for we have no might against this great company that cometh against us; neither know we what to do: but our eyes are upon thee.
>
> 2 Chronicles 20:11, 12

What kind of war plan is that? No program, no committee action. No flying banners, no bright and shiny war machinery, no brilliant war plans. No blaring of trumpets or mustering of patriotic armies. Just a simple confession: "We are in this over our heads. We don't know what to do, so we will just keep our eyes on the Lord." They decided to stand still, admit their confusion, and put all their eggs in one basket. They would not move anywhere but closer to their Lord; they would look no other place for help but to Him.

Does it all sound cowardly and ridiculous? Well-armed enemy troops surrounded them, and vultures filled the skies, waiting for the battle to begin. They just stood together, praising God, admitting they didn't know what to do next, and looked only to Him for deliverance.

Nowadays when we get into trouble, we act as if we are saying, "Lord, I love you, but I already know what I'm going to do." When the enemy comes in like a flood, we panic. We feel *we* must do something, make something move or give. We have a need to see things happen, and we feel guilty if we are not constantly proving to God how willing we are to do anything He requires of us.

The Urge to "Make Things Happen" Comes to Us All

A divorced mother worried about her little boy's insecurity since his dad left the home. The child wouldn't let his mother out of his sight. He screamed and called for his daddy. All the love this mother showered on him didn't seem to be enough. What did this Christian mother do? She called her friends for advice. She researched books on child raising, looking for solutions. She went about her day in worrisome concern, thinking to herself, "I've just got to do something about this problem, before it gets out of hand."

There is a better way. It's absolutely scriptural for that mother to throw up her hands and cry, "It's too much for me;

I've tried my best; I don't know whom to turn to or what to do. No one can help me, so I'll just stay close to Jesus, keep my eyes only on Him, and trust He will see me through."

A perplexed couple was on the verge of giving up. They wanted to give 100 percent to Jesus, but they had been exposed to legalistic preaching of fear, which had brought them under bondage. They got swept up into the Charismatic Movement, hoping to find joy and fulfillment. One preacher warned them, "Jesus says you must be perfect. He would never ask us to do something we couldn't do. To say you must sin a little each day is a cop-out." Another preacher said, "If you are not one hundred percent obedient, Jesus cannot save you." Another added, "Delayed obedience is disobedience. Any disobedience can damn you." Now they worry about all the things they forgot to do, about their imperfections and daily battles with the flesh, and they feel defeated.

Recently they picked up an evangelist's newsletter which warned:

> On Judgment Day there will be many Christians who have been to church three times a week, prayed in tongues, given prophecies, taught Sunday School, and served as deacons, who have not read their Bibles enough and prayed enough. God is angry with people who sin every day. He is determined to punish them eternally. There is no hope unless they stop sinning completely.

Now they also worry about not having prayed, given, and read their Bibles enough to please God. They live in constant fear. They have been told various things about their fear. Some claimed a "demon of fear" had crept into them. Others told them they were guilty of a "wrong confession," and they were urged "not to accept that fear." "Just confess victory," they were told, "and all will be well."

The wife said, "We have become so miserable in our efforts to clean ourselves up for God. Every night we evaluate our day and always feel God is displeased, because we somehow failed to behave right, confess right, or do right. We promise to do better tomorrow, but these are the things that make us want to give up and quit trying. We've lost our sense of peace and security. This is not the abundant life; it is fear. Doesn't the cross of Jesus mean more than that?"

What should they do? They wonder now who is right—the Charismatics or the Baptists. Their faith is shaken, and they have lost their sense of direction. Which teacher is right? They all seem to have such good arguments and plenty of Scriptures to prove their points. What is holiness? What does God expect? Did God do it all for me at the cross, or do I have to muster up my own strength and work out my own salvation with fear and trembling? It's very confusing!

My answer: Admit your confusion. Don't seek out pat answers to all these questions. Don't run around looking for teachers to give you solutions and answers. You don't know what to do or where to go? Good! Very good! Now you are ready to do it God's way. Now you can say with Paul, "I've decided to know nothing among you but Christ and him crucified" (*see* 1 Corinthians 2:2). Quit looking to these preachers and teachers; go yourself to the Lord. Get your eyes on Him, and, with Jehoshaphat, cry aloud: "My eyes are fixed on You!"

A couple in Iowa are trying to save their marriage. They have been married fifteen years, and the last five have been unbearable. Both have skeletons in their closets, and both have been guilty of taking their vows lightly. He cheated, and she "almost did." For five years they have tried to forgive each other, but the marriage is not fulfilling now. They pledge their love to each other, but each of them knows something is wrong. They can't put their fingers on it; they are lonely, even when together. They are not reaching each other, and the harder they try, the more frustrated they become. They'll have a good week, when everything seems to be patched up and going well; then suddenly it all breaks down, and silent anger and resentment take over. She cries herself to sleep; he thinks of giving up. In a way, they are still attracted to each other. In another way, they seem to be allergic to each other. They have tried to talk their problems through; they have made promises they couldn't keep; they have read books, seeking help; they have been to a marriage counselor. But nothing brings about an honest solution. They have both reached a place where there is no turning back. They simply do not know what to do or where to go for help.

Is there any solution? I think so. All marriages, even good ones, have their periods of stress. But some marriages can't be healed at all, outside of genuine miracles. When two people have tried everything, when it dawns on them that there is no place to go for help, when confusion and panic take over, that is when God has to intervene. Once again, all you can do in such a crisis is do as King Jehoshaphat. Don't be afraid of your confusion. You aren't the only one up against a wall. God specializes in hopeless cases. God takes over when we give up trying to work it all out ourselves. This couple with a marriage about to hit the rocks must stop looking for help outside of the Lord. They must commit their problems and their lives over to the Lord and pray, "God, it's over our heads. We've tried and failed. It looks hopeless, so we'll just stand in Your presence and look only to You for help. It's You, Lord, or nothing. Our eyes will stay fixed on You."

Reader, you too face crises in which you don't know what to do or where to go for help. What about you? Is it a financial crisis staring you right in the face? Do you live in a home situation which tears your spirit apart? Have your children hurt you, or has a child brought anguish to you? Has sickness or pain brought you down to the valley of death? Have you lost a job? Is your future scary and uncertain? Is *your* marriage in trouble? Has the death of a loved one left you depressed, lonely, and empty? Has a divorce left you feeling like a rejected failure?

Do you feel overwhelmed right now? Have you tried so many ways to see it through, yet nothing seems to help? Have you grown tired of trying? Have you almost decided there is no way out? Have you reached the end of your rope? Have you said to your heart, "I don't know what to do now!"?

We are living in a time when everything is getting shaky and insecure, and almost everybody is hurting in one way or another.

Hardly anybody knows what to do anymore. Our leaders don't have the foggiest idea of what is happening to this world or to the economy. The future is anybody's guess.

The business world is even more confused; economists are arguing with each other about what is coming. There is not a single businessman or economist in the world today who knows for certain where we are headed.

Psychologists and psychiatrists are baffled by the changing forces affecting people today. They watch the breakup of homes and marriages and become as confused as the rest of us as to why it is happening. Their reasons contradict each other.

It can even be confusing for Christians nowadays. Ministers admonish us to face our problems by looking into the Bible for ourselves, finding our own answers. But the Bible doesn't always specify "this you must do!" There is not always a direct answer for your specific problem. At times, unless the Spirit gives you a special revelation, you can get confused by verses which seem, on the surface, to be contradictory. At one place you read, "Sell all you have and give to the poor." Then you read, "If a man neglect his own house, he is worse than an infidel and has denied the faith." If you sold all and gave it away to the poor, how could you have any left to provide well for your own?

Believe it or not, even the greatest saints who ever lived did not fully understand the battle between the flesh and the spirit. Why do we have all these denominations? Why is there all the fighting over doctrine? Why are there so many disputes over baptisms, doctrines, and morals? Simply because men today are still confused and uncertain. You may think your church has all the answers, the whole truth and nothing but the truth. But it is not so! No one has it all! We are still in darkness about so many things. We all eventually reach a place, as King Jehoshaphat did. The enemy comes against us all. Some put on a big front, as though they have no fears, no questions, no problems; but they are the ones who inwardly fight the worst battles. Often those who judge everybody else and who appear so holy and righteous before others are waging a war with lust, deep inside.

Yes, we are all hurting in one way or another. We are all in need. We all reach that point of panic when the heart cries out, "What do I do now?"

Some people think I should not confess that I, too, have battles. But I do get spiritually dry at times. I do get plunged into darkness and confusion, on occasion. With Joseph, I can confess, "The Word tries me." I am no better or worse than any reader of this book. The saintliest people hurt, too. I know what King Jehoshaphat was going through. I've been there, when I had to cry aloud, "I don't know what to do, so I'll keep my eyes fixed on Him!"

You don't fold your hands, sit around at ease, and let God do it all! That is not what it means to keep your eyes fixed on the Lord. We look to the Lord, not as people who know what to do, but as people who do not know at all what they must do. We do know God is the King who sits on the flood. He is Lord of all, and we know, even if the world breaks in two, even if it all falls apart, He is a Rock of certainty. Our eyes are fixed on a risen Lord. If we do not know what to do, our faith assures us He knows what to do.

Dietrich Bonhoeffer, the German theologian, pictured the Christian as someone trying to cross a sea of floating pieces of ice. This Christian cannot rest anywhere while crossing, except in his faith that God will see him through. He cannot stand anywhere too long, or he will sink. After taking a step, he must watch out for the next step. Beneath him is the abyss, and before him is uncertainty, but always ahead of him is the Lord, firm and sure! He doesn't see the land yet, but it is there—a promise in his heart. So the Christian traveler keeps his eyes fixed upon his final place.

I prefer to think of life as more abundant and joyful than that. I picture life as a wilderness journey like that of the children of Israel. And I picture King Jehoshaphat's battle, along with all the children of Judah, as our battle. Sure, it's a wilderness. Yes, there are snakes, dry water holes, valleys of tears, enemy armies, hot sands, drought, and impassable mountains. But when the children of the Lord stood still to see His salvation, He spread a table in that wilderness and rained manna from above. He destroyed enemy armies by His power alone. He brought water out of rocks, took the poison out of snakebites, refreshed them with rain and dew, led them by pillar and cloud, gave them milk and honey, and brought them into a promised land, with a high and mighty hand. God warned them to tell every following generation: ". . . Not by might, nor by power, but by my spirit, saith the Lord of hosts" (Zechariah 4:6).

A reporter asked me to respond to a question about pressures on the church from the IRS and other government agencies. "Isn't the IRS trying to tax all evangelical ministries? Won't that day come when the government will strangle missionary and evangelical outreaches? What will you do then, seeing that these things are already in the works?"

I replied: "We are going to be forced right back into doing the work of Jesus the way He did it Himself. The day will probably come when I and all my minister friends will have to quit doing evangelism like big business and get back to New Testament methods. We will be priced out of expensive methods and go back to walking the streets with sinners, as Jesus did. As long as our eyes are focused on Jesus, no one will ever stop His message from being preached."

That Is Why Jesus Said, "I Am the Way!"

Stop searching! Stop looking in the wrong direction for help. Get alone with Jesus in a secret place; tell Him all about your confusion. Tell Him you have no other place to go. Tell Him you trust Him alone to see you through. You will be tempted to take matters into your own hands. You will want to figure things out on your own. You will wonder whether God is working at all; there will be no sign of things changing. Your faith will be tested to the limit. But nothing else works, anyway, so there is nothing to lose. Peter summed it all up: ". . . to whom shall we go? thou hast the words of eternal life" (John 6:68).

> Looking unto Jesus the author and finisher of our faith. . . .
>
> Hebrews 12:2

> Look unto me, and be ye saved, all the ends of the earth: for I am God, and there is none else.
>
> Isaiah 45:22

> . . . ye that seek the Lord: look unto the rock whence ye are hewn. . . .
>
> Isaiah 51:1

Therefore I will look unto the Lord; I will wait for the God of my salvation: my God will hear me.

Micah 7:7

He shall not be afraid of evil tidings: his heart is fixed, trusting in the Lord.

Psalms 112:7

Who is among you that feareth the Lord, that obeyeth the voice of his servant, that walketh in darkness, and hath no light? let him trust in the name of the Lord, and stay upon his God.

Isaiah 50:10

11

God Can Use You

in Spite of Your Weaknesses

God has determined to accomplish His goals, here on earth, through men with weaknesses. Isaiah, the great prayer warrior, was a man of like passions, which means he, just like the rest of us, was weak and wounded. David, the man after God's own heart, was a murdering adulterer who had no moral right to any of God's blessings. Peter denied the very Lord God of heaven, cursing the One who loved him most. Abraham, the father of nations, lived a lie, using his wife as a pawn to save his own skin. Jacob was a conniver. Paul was impatient and harsh with converts and associates who could not live up to his ascetic life-style. Adam and Eve turned a perfect marriage arrangement into a nightmare. Solomon, the wisest man on earth, did some of the most stupid things ever recorded in history. Samuel murdered King Agag in a rage of anger, in an overzealous show of righteousness. Joseph taunted his lost brothers in almost boyish glee, until the games almost backfired on him. Jonah wanted to see an entire city burn, to justify his prophecies against it; he despised the mercy of God toward a repentant people. Lot offered his two virgin daughters to a mob of sex-crazed Sodomites.

The list of men who loved God, men who were greatly used

by God, who were almost driven to the ground by their weaknesses, goes on and on. Yet God was always there, saying, "I called you; I will be with you! I will take away the evil of your heart! I will accomplish my will, regardless!"

God's Treasure Is in Earthen Vessels

One of the most encouraging Scriptures in the Bible is 2 Corinthians 4:7: "But we have this treasure in earthen vessels, that the excellency of the power may be of God, and not of us." Then Paul goes on to describe those earthen vessels as dying men, troubled on every side, perplexed, persecuted, cast down. Even though never forsaken or in despair, those men used by God were constantly groaning under the burden of their bodies, waiting anxiously to be clothed with new ones.

God mocks man's power. He laughs at our egotistical efforts at being good. He never uses the high and mighty, but instead He uses the weak things of this world to confound the wise.

> For ye see your calling, brethren, how that not many wise men after the flesh, not many mighty, not many noble, are called: But God hath chosen the foolish things of the world to confound the wise; and God hath chosen the weak things of the world to confound the things which are mighty; And base things of the world, and things which are despised, hath God chosen, yea, and things which are not. . . . That no flesh should glory in his presence.
>
> 1 Corinthians 1:26–29

Wow! Does that ever describe me! Weak thing! Foolish thing! Despised thing! A base thing! A thing not very noble, not very smart, not very mighty! What insanity to think God could use such a creature! Yet that is His perfect plan and the greatest mystery on earth. God calls us in our weaknesses, even when He knows we'll do it wrong. He puts His priceless treasure in these earthen vessels of ours, because He delights in doing the impossible with nothing.

God Delights in Using Failures

God delights in using men and women who think of themselves as unable to do anything right. A woman wrote to me recently, saying:

> I'm the world's number-one failure. My marriage is failing. I seem to do everything wrong in raising my children. I'm not very good at anything. I'm not even able to understand the Bible very well. Most of it is over my head. I feel as though I'm not worth anything to anyone. I've not been a very good wife, mother, or Christian. I have to be the world's greatest failure.

She is just the kind of person the Lord is looking for: a person who knows that if anything good happens through her, it has to be God. All the hotshot Christians who go about bowling people over with their great abilities never impress God. He looked down on a scheming, base, weakling of a man called Jacob and said: "Fear not, thou worm Jacob . . . I will help thee. . . . Behold, I will make thee a new sharp threshing instrument having teeth . . . thou shalt rejoice in the Lord . . ." (Isaiah 41:14–16).

Men often use God to achieve fortune, fame, honor, and respect. Talent, personality, and cleverness are all used to advance God's kingdom, but God is not impressed. His strength is perfected in those of weakness.

When I Say Weakness, I Do Not Mean Sensuality

God does *not* use people weak in righteousness. A man's weakness can lead him into adultery, gambling, drinking, and all kinds of indulgences. God is not referring to that kind of weakness. When He calls the base, He is not referring to the wicked.

The weakness God speaks about is our human inability to obey His commandments in our own strength. God calls us to a life of holiness and separation. He tells us we can be free from the bondage of sin. His Word promises freedom from sin's power, as well as forgiveness. God's Word comes to us with some impossible challenges: "Resist the devil! Walk in the Spirit! Come out from among them! Do not commit adultery! Love your enemies! Enter into rest! Leave behind all your fears! Put down your lustful desires! Let no sin have dominion over you! As He was in this world, so be ye! Overcome self, pride, and envy! Sin not!"

Do you know how to answer that call? Think honestly about how little you can do, on your own, to fulfill these challenges; then you will realize how very weak you are. Your heart begins to cry, "Lord, how can we do such great, holy things? How are these things possible?" There is no way at all you can stand up to these commandments and challenges in your own strength and knowledge. The call to holiness is frightening and disturbing. You know what God asks of you, but you don't seem to know how to fulfill it.

Some think they can do it on their own, so they go into a convulsive concentration of all their inner resources. They grit their teeth and muster up all their human powers. They set out with great energy and resolve, calling upon all they have and taking matters into their own hands. They proceed to obey, or die trying. It works for a little while, until God crosses them up. He steps in and foils all men's schemes and self-determined efforts of the flesh. Then failure strikes, just at the moment all seemed to be going so well. These do-it-yourself Christians end up frustrated, defenseless, and weak.

That is when our Lord takes over! He comes with such a

comforting message: "Lay down your weapons. Quit trying to be so self-sufficient and strong. I am your weapon, your only weapon. I am your strength. Let Me do what you can never do. You are not supposed to do it on your own; I must do it, so you will glorify only Me. I will give you My righteousness, My holiness, My rest, and My strength. You can't save yourself; you can't help yourself; you can't please Me in any way, except by receiving the blessings of the cross, by faith. Let Me be in charge of your growth in holiness."

If You Have Too Much Going for You, God Can't Work!

Gideon is an example of a called man who had too much going for him. He was called to deliver God's children from slavery. What did he do? He blasted the trumpets and called together a mighty army. Thousands of valiant fighting men rallied under his banner, but God said to Gideon, "Your army is too great; you have too many men, too much strength. Send them back. If you win the victory with all this show of strength, you and your people might think you won on your own abilities. You have too much going for you, and I don't want you to steal the glory. Strip down your army!"

One by one, those men left Gideon's army. He must have stood by thinking, "How ridiculous! Win by weakening ourselves? God calls me to do battle, then asks me to disarm. Insanity! This is the craziest thing God has yet asked me to do. There goes my plan to become a legend in my own time."

Those fighters must have left the battlefield, shuddering with astonishment. Who ever heard of winning a battle by laying aside weapons and manpower?

From a human standpoint, it is crazy to have great victories by tiny remnants, walls tumbled without a shot fired, armies put to flight by a motley orchestra of trumpet players. By the power of faith alone, weak men confound the world.

The Way to Holiness Is Humility

No matter how powerful and honorable a man may be, God cannot use him, until he falls in the dust and gives up all his idols. Human pride must be smashed. All our boasting must be silenced. All our thoughts and plans must be abandoned. All human achievement must be recognized for what it is: filthy rags and a stench in God's nostrils.

Man must become powerless, defenseless, and hopeless in himself. He must come with fear and trembling to the cross and cry out, "Be Thou Lord of my life."

There Is Also a Weakness of the Flesh

There are Christians who fail the Lord. They love Him very much; they worry about grieving Him; but, in spite of their love and good intentions, they fall into sin. Even ministers commit adultery. Multitudes of Christians fight inner battles with lust. Their passions overrun them, and they become victims to overwhelming desires. There are modern Bathshebas and Delilahs, as well as men of God who are enticed and deceived by them.

Some of these weak children of the Lord are guilty of the sin of Peter: They have denied the Lord who called them. Others are weighed down by the guilt and condemnation of secret sins. Only God knows the battles that are fought by men and women who are among the most esteemed in the church. Those with the most acute battles often spend much of their time crying out against the sins of others, mostly to divert attention from their own struggle with the flesh.

Does God quit on any child of His who is waging a war against some white-hot passion? Does God lift His Spirit before the victory is won? Does the Lord stand nearby watching, as if to say: "You know what I expect of you. You know My laws and My commandments. When you get it right, when you wiggle free from your lust, then I'll set in motion your river of blessings. Until then, you are on your own"?

Never! Never! Instead, our Lord comes to us in our weakest moment, with sin stains blotched all over our garments, and He whispers, "My strength is for you in this your hour of weakness. Don't give up. Don't panic. Don't turn away. Don't shut Me out. Is there godly sorrow in you? Do you despise what you did? Do you want victory? Keep moving with Me. Keep moving toward Me. My arms are still stretched out, as a mother hen spreading her wings. Come, I'll protect you from the enemy."

People are giving up because they feel so weak before the power of the enemy. They say to themselves, "Why doesn't God come down and take this ugly thing out of me?"

We seem to forget God often leads us the long way around; we are seldom permitted to march straight into the Promised Land. There are lessons on faith to be learned. The wilderness temptations give God a way to show His power to deliver. Only Christians who have come through hurt, fires of temptation, and agony of defeat can really help others who hurt.

I saw Israel Narvaez, former Mau Mau gang leader, kneel and receive Christ as Lord. It was not just an emotional, surface experience; he really meant it. But Israel went back to the gang and ended up in prison as an accessory to murder. Did God quit on him? Not for one moment! Today Israel is a minister of the Gospel, having accepted the love and forgiveness of a long-suffering Saviour.

Have you failed? Is there a sin that so easily besets you? Do you feel like a weakened coward, unable to get the victory over secret sin? With that weakness in you, is there also a consuming hunger for God? Do you yearn for Him, love Him, reach to Him? That hunger and thirst is the key to your victory! That makes you different from all others who have been guilty of failing God. That sets you apart. You must keep that hunger alive. You must keep thirsting after righteousness. Never justify your weakness; never give in to it; never accept it as a part of your life.

There Is Only One Thing That Works

Faith is your victory. Abraham had weaknesses: He lied, and he almost turned his wife into an adulteress, but Abraham ". . . believed God, and it was counted unto him for righteousness" (Romans 4:3). God refused to hold his sin against him, because he believed.

Sure, you have failed—maybe yesterday, or today. Grievously! Shamefully! But do you believe Jesus has the power to ultimately free you from sin's power? Do you believe the cross of Jesus means sin's bondage is broken? Do you accept the fact that He has promised to deliver you from the snare (trap) of Satan?

Let me tell you exactly where I believe the victory is. Let your faith rise. Let your heart accept all the promises of victory in Jesus. Then let your faith tell your heart, "I may not be what I want to be yet, but God is at work in me, and He has the power to loose sin's hold on me. I'm going to keep my momentum toward the Lord, until I'm free at last. It may be little by little, but the day will come when faith will conquer. I will not always be a slave. I am not the devil's puppet. I am a weak child of God, wanting the strength of Jesus. I am not going to be another victim of the devil. I am going to come forth as pure gold, tried in the fire. God is for me. I commit it all to Him who is able to keep me from falling and present me faultless before the throne of God with exceeding great joy."

12

God Has Not Forgotten You

There is a fiery message burning in my bones. It is a message every Christian needs to hear, especially in this age of overpowering temptation and excruciating hurt.

The message I bring you from the Lord is simply this: *God has not forgotten you!* He knows exactly where you are and what you are going through right now, and He is monitoring every step along your path. But we are just as the children of Israel, who doubted God's daily care for them, even though prophets were sent to deliver wonderful promises from heaven.

God's people sat in darkness, hungry and thirsty, praying for deliverance and comfort. God bottled every tear, and He heard their cry and answered, "I will preserve you. . . . You shall no longer hunger and thirst. . . . I will have mercy on you and lead you by springs of living water . . . for the Lord will comfort his people and have mercy on all the troubled ones" (*see* Isaiah 49). Did Israel rejoice in these promises sent directly from the throne of God? Did God's people quit their fretting and begin trusting in the Lord to see them through? Did those who were hurt and confused believe a single word of these promises? "No! "But Zion said, The Lord hath forsaken me, and my Lord hath forgotten me" (Isaiah 49:14).

These were not reprobates or sons of the devil. Rather,

they were those "who sought the Lord . . . the sons of Abraham . . . those who knew righteousness . . . in whose heart was the law of God. . . ." How much clearer must God make His Word to these stubborn, unbelieving children? God was greatly concerned because they were not appropriating or hearing His promises. You can almost sense the impatience of the Lord in rebuking their unbelief:

> I, even I, am he that comforteth you: who art thou, that thou shouldest be afraid of a man. . . . And forgettest the Lord thy maker, that hath stretched forth the heavens, and laid the foundations of the earth; and hast feared continually every day because of the fury of the oppressor, as if he were ready to destroy? . . ."
>
> Isaiah 51:12, 13

We Simply Ignore God's Promises

Does it all sound familiar? Here we are today, as children of the same holy God, having in us the glorious promise of Holy Ghost comfort; yet we go about, daily, fearing the oppressor. We know what our Lord has promised us: guidance, peace, a shelter from the storm, a way where there seems to be none, a supply for every need, healing for every hurt. Do we believe any of it? Do we just put these promises out of our minds and go on our ways, worrying and fretting and taking matters into our own hands? I'm afraid so! And we are all alike. We get in a tight place; we get lonely and depressed; we fall into temptation and yield to lust; we make tragic errors and live in guilt and terror; and through it all, we choose to forget all God has promised us. We forget we serve a God who laid the very foundations of this earth. We forget our Father is all-powerful, and all things which exist were made by Him. We see only our problems. Our fears shut out the vision of His power and glory. We get afraid; we panic; we question; we doubt.

We forget, in our hour of need, that God has us in the palm of His hand. Instead, as the children of Israel, we are afraid we are going to blow it all and be destroyed by the enemy. How difficult it must be for our loving Father to understand why we won't trust Him when we are down and in need. God must think to Himself, "Don't they know I have graven them upon the palms of My hands? I could no more forget them in their hour of need than a mother could forget her suckling child . . . and even though a mother could forget her child, I cannot forget a single child of Mine" (*see* Isaiah 49:15, 16).

The Sin of Christians Is Unbelief

Again and again God came to Israel, pleading for their confidence and trust in times of crises. "For thus saith the Lord God, the Holy One of Israel; In returning and rest shall ye be saved; in quietness and in confidence shall be your strength: and *ye would not*" (Isaiah 30:15, *italics mine*). God said to them, "You didn't ask at My mouth or pray for help and guidance. You didn't wait for Me to help. You didn't return to Me for help and strength when you really needed it. You didn't accept My counsel; you didn't wait for Me to work. You didn't wait for that quiet word behind you that whispers, 'This is the way; walk ye in it.' You didn't believe My strong arm could deliver you. You didn't call upon My name or rest in the shadow of My palm. No! You took matters in your own hands; you depended on others; you trusted in your own thoughts. You conceived chaff and were burnt by your own fire."

God seems finally to shout at Israel:

Seek ye out of the book of the Lord, and read: no one [promise] . . . shall fail . . . for my mouth it hath com-

manded. . . . Strengthen ye the weak hands, and con-
firm the feeble knees. Say to them that are of a fearful
heart, Be strong, fear not: behold, your God will come
with vengeance, even God with a recompence; he will
come and save you. . . . Sorrow and sighing shall flee
away.

> Isaiah 34:16; 35:3, 4, 10

It seems to me even the New Testament echoes God's
displeasure with unbelief:

. . . ask in faith, nothing wavering. For he that
wavereth is like a wave of the sea driven with the wind
and tossed. For let not that man think that he shall receive any thing of the Lord. A double minded man is
unstable in all his ways.

> James 1:6–8

Jesus was concerned that when He returned to this earth,
He would not find any faith left. He had just finished a
message about how certainly God answers prayer. He had
just promised that the heavenly Father would speedily
". . . avenge [and answer] his own elect, which cry day and
night unto him . . ." (Luke 18(7). It must have been with a
heavy heart that Jesus spoke the following: "I tell you that he
will avenge them speedily. Nevertheless when the Son of
man cometh, shall he find faith on the earth?" (Luke 18:8).

We Have Begun to Doubt That God Still Answers Prayer

Can it be that we continue in our hurt, in our sin, or in
living in defeat and failure, simply because we really do not
believe God answers our prayers anymore?

Are we as guilty as the children of Israel in thinking God
has forgotten us? Are we acting as though the Lord has forsak-

en us and given us over to our own devices, to figure things
out for ourselves? Do .we really believe our Lord meant it
when He said God will act just in time, in answer to our
prayer of faith? Jesus implies that most of us, even though
called and chosen, will not be trusting in Him when He re-
turns. Some of God's people have already lost their confidence in Him. They do not believe, in the deepest part of
their souls, that their prayers make any difference. They act as
if they are all on their own.

Instead of submitting to the Lord in quiet confidence and
resting in His promises, we try so hard to work out our own
solutions. Then when our way of doing things blows up in our
faces, we get angry with God.

A young divorcée confessed, "I almost went out to get stone
drunk tonight. I've been praying for a whole year now for my
husband to return, but, instead of coming back to me, he has
taken up with another woman. God didn't answer my prayer,
so I thought I'd go out and get drunk to show Him how angry I
am." What a pity! She was ready to take it out on God because
He wouldn't answer her prayer her way, on her time
schedule. Like so many others who beg God for favors, she
wanted only one thing: relief from her loneliness and release
for her sexual drive. She didn't want more of Jesus or more
holiness and Christian character. No! She simply wanted a man
at her side. I knew immediately that God could not answer
that woman's prayer. She was not ready to receive her husband back. She was still an emotional cripple, and she would
blow it a second time. Then all she would have left would be
another failure, and her despair would be compounded. God
had not forsaken her; He was actually being merciful to her.
He was saving her life, but she couldn't see it.

Be honest now! Has your faith been weak lately? Have you
almost given up on certain things you have prayed so much
about? Have you grown weary with waiting? Have you thrown

up your hands in resignation, as if to say, "I just can't seem to break through. I don't know what is wrong or why my prayer is not answered. Evidently God has said no to me."

What about all the lonely people in the world who are torn apart by their solitude? What about the young, unmarried people who spend months and even years praying for a loving mate? Others would be satisfied if God would answer prayer and give them just a friend. They cry at night. The telephone becomes their lifeline, and when things get unbearable, they call someone—anyone—just to talk for a while. Does God still answer that kind of prayer? You know—the old-fashioned kind where Christian girls still pray for Christian husbands and Christian boys pray for Christian wives? Can God miraculously send friends and mates into lonely lives, in answer to prayer and faith? I still have to believe God works that way. Yet I know for a fact, after interviewing hundreds of lonely people, that few of them really believe God's promises.

Show me a lonely, hurting child of God who puts character and growth ahead of all other needs, and I'll show you one who is sure to be fulfilled. Instead of praying with faith, instead of quietly trusting His promises, instead of reading God's Word and growing in strength, instead of committing their futures to His keeping—most lonely people watch TV, read junk magazines, and grow spiritually dull. Their faith is weak because they are spiritually crippled. They pray only in quick snatches. They wallow in self-pity and self-condemnation. They are stunted and unbelieving, ready to think God has picked them out of the crowd to be treated wrongly. God can't answer their prayers, because they are not ready for friendship and true love. They would mess it up in a short time because unbelief with God always leads to instability in human relationships. I say to all lonely people: Get back to the secret closet! Get back to simple, childlike faith! Start yearning for Jesus more than for friends or mates. God will, according to His own Word, meet your every need.

God, Help Me, or I'm Going to Blow It All

Almost everywhere I go today, I hear Christians, even ministers, tell me there is something missing in their lives. A pastor friend summed it up like this: "David, I start to hunger after the Lord. I get a broken spirit; I weep and cry for hours. I feel as if something in me is seeking expression, as though a birth is about to take place. I want more from God and more out of life. I want to be holy. I want to know God and get through to Him. I pray that what I feel won't dissipate but will keep growing until I break through. But, sadly, in a few weeks, I lose my broken spirit. I go back to my old fears and dryness. I get so close, but I never go all the way. Then I say to myself, 'What happened?' "

Does that describe what you go through? Do you feel as if you are just outside the gates, so close, and about to break through to a life of joy, faith, answered prayers, and victory? Is there something in you that keeps condemning you, as if you never do enough to please God? At times do you think to yourself, "I'm just not doing anything. I'm not getting anything accomplished. I'm not growing. I'm not making real progress"?

I am of the opinion that, in all of us, just beneath the surface, there lingers a horrible thought: *Oh, God, help me, or I'm going to blow it all.* We never say it, but we think it: *God, I'm so weak, so susceptible to my besetting sin, so ignorant about winning over temptation, so confused about prayer and how to overcome the devil. I'm afraid I'll do something stupid and ruin everything.*

God Is Not a Divine Tease or Riddle

What does it all mean when prayers go unanswered, when hurts linger, when suffering is permitted to continue, and God seems to be doing nothing in response to our faith? Often God is loving us more supremely at those times than ever

before. The Word says, ". . . whom the Lord loveth he chas-
teneth . . ." (Hebrews 12:6). A chastening of love takes pre-
cedence over every act of faith, over every prayer, over every
promise. What I see as hurting in me could be His loving me.
It could be His gentle hand spanking me out of my stubborn-
ness and pride. God could be saying to me, "I've promised to
meet your every need. I told you I would do anything you
asked of Me in faith. You need to submit to a season of chastening; it is the only way I can make you into an experienced
vessel of love. You may ask to be delivered, but it will only
delay your spiritual growth. Through this suffering you will
learn obedience, if you submit."

We have faith in our faith. We place more emphasis on the
power of our prayers than we do on getting His power into us.
We want to figure out God, so we can read Him like a book.
We don't want to be surprised or bewildered. And when
things happen contrary to our concept of God, we say, "That
can't be God; that's not the way He works."

We are so busy working on God, we forget He is trying to
work on us. That is what this life is all about: God at work on
us, trying to remake us into vessels of glory. We are so busy
praying to change things that we have little time to allow
prayer to change us. God has not put prayer and faith in our
hands as if they were two secret tools by which a select group
of "experts" learn to pray something out of Him. God said He
is more willing to give than we are to receive. Why are we
using prayer and faith as keys or tools to unlock something
that has never been locked up? It's all freely given. It's been
outpoured. It's a storehouse with all the doors and windows
opened, with a Father who is already at work, daily loading us
with His benefits. When Jesus said, "Knock, and it shall be
opened," He was talking about our doors, not His. Knock
down all our own doors. We need no key to enter His presence.

Beloved bride of Christ, is that not the way we treat our Master? We demand the use of His credit cards, while showing so little interest in His love. All the promises are given to us so we can become partakers of Him. He wants to get His divine nature of love into our puny bodies.

Do I believe all the promises are mine? Yes! Do I believe God still answers prayer? Yes! Do I believe He will comfort me, deliver me, give me the things I need to be free and fulfilled? Yes! But all God does in me and for me depends on this one thing: I must believe He hears me when I call! He bottles every tear; He is more willing to give than I am to receive; He is most anxious to answer every prayer that will help me be more like Himself; and He will never withhold anything I need any longer than I can bear to be without it.

God has not forsaken you or me. No! A thousand times no! Right now He is wanting us all to believe He is working all things out for our good. So quit trying to figure it out! Stop worrying! Stop doubting our Lord! The answer is coming! God has not shut His ear. We will reap—in due season—if we faint not!

Prayer is not for God's benefit; it is for ours. Faith is no
His benefit, but for ours. God is not some eternal, di
tease. He has not surrounded Himself with riddles for me
unravel, as if to say, "The wise will get the prize."

We are so mixed up on this matter of prayer and faith.
have had the audacity to think of God as our personal ge
who fulfills every wish. We think of faith as a way to cor
God on His promises. We think God is pleased by our eff
to back Him against the wall and shout, "Lord, You can't
back on Your promise. I want what is coming to me. You
bound by Your Word. You must do it, or Your Word is
true."

This is why we miss the true meaning of prayer and fai
We see God only as the Giver and ourselves as the receive
But prayer and faith are the avenues by which we become t
givers to God. They are to be used, not as ways to get thin
from God, but as ways to give Him those things by which v
can please Him.

Something Better Than Answered Prayer

Do you want a promise, or do you want the Promisemake
Do you want answers to prayer, or do you want Him wl
works all things together for good?

Can you imagine a wife who sticks with her husband on
for the benefits she receives? She enjoys the prestige of h
renowned husband, and she freely uses his name to enhan
her own position. She enjoys all the luxuries he provides; s
constantly spends on his credit cards. Yet she takes 1
granted the one who loves her so. She has little time to spe
with him; she is so preoccupied with her own comfort a
pleasure. How long before the world knows she uses l
husband, that she is interested, not so much in him, but
what he provides?

13

"Will God Ever Answer My Prayer?"

Have you ever asked that question? Is there one special matter you have been praying about for a long time, with no apparent answer in sight? Are there times when you wonder if the answer will ever come? Have you honestly done everything you know you should do? Have you fulfilled every requirement of prayer? Have you wept, fasted, and fervently petitioned God in true faith? And yet nothing seems to happen? If you must answer yes to all the above questions, you are in good company. You are not some strange kind of Christian, suffering chastisement from the Lord. The delayed answer to prayer is one of the most common experiences shared by even the saintliest of God's children.

I thank God for ministers and teachers who preach faith. So do I! Thank God for teachers who stir my soul to expect miracles and answers to all my prayers. Perhaps the church has become so faithless and unbelieving that God has to give us an explosive, new, and fresh revelation of His powerful promises.

There is much new teaching today on "making the right confession." Also, God's people are being urged to think positively and affirm all the promises of God. We are told to rid our lives of all hidden grudges—make all our wrongs right, even back to childhood. Lately, it has been taught that most of

our unanswered prayers, our lingering illnesses, our inability
to move God on our own behalf is a direct result of mishan-
dling our faith. As one faith teacher put it, "Faith is like a
faucet; you can turn it off or on."

It all sounds so simple. Do you need a financial miracle in
your life? Then you are told, simply rid your life of all the
hindrances, grudges, and unbelief. Confess to having already
received the answer, by faith, and it will be yours. Do you
want that divorced husband to return for a reconciliation?
Confess it, imagine it is happening, create a mental image of a
beautiful reunion, and it is all yours. Is there someone you
love, who is at death's door? Then put God on notice that you
will not take no for an answer; remind Him of His promises;
confess healing; and it will happen, so it is taught. And if your
prayer is not answered, if the husband stays away for months
on end, if the sick loved one dies, if the financial need turns
into a crisis, it is suggested that it is all your fault. Somewhere
along the line, you allowed a negative thought to block the
channel. Or you had a secret sin or unsurrendered grudge.
Your confession was unscriptural or insincere. One faith
teacher wrote, "If you didn't get the results I did, you aren't
doing everything I did!"

I am not being facetious. I believe God answers prayer. Oh,
how I do believe that! But my office is receiving tragic letters
from honest Christians who are totally confused and despon-
dent, because they can't seem to make all these new prayer-
and-faith formulas work. "What's wrong with me?" writes one
troubled lady. "I've searched my heart and have confessed
every sin. I've bound demonic powers by the Word of God.
I've fasted; I've prayed; I've confessed the promises—yet, I
have not seen the answer. I must be spiritually blind, or I'm
doing it all wrong."

Believe me, there are thousands of confused Christians, all
across this nation, who are condemning themselves for not

being able to produce an answer to a desperate prayer. They know God's Word is true, that not a single promise can fail, that God is faithful to all generations, that He is good, and that He wants His children to expect answers to their prayers. Yet, for them, there is that one prayer that goes unanswered—indefinitely. So they blame themselves. They listen to the tapes of teachers and preachers who speak so powerfully and positively about all the answers they are getting as a result of their faith. And they hear the testimonies of others who have a formula all worked out and who now receive all they ask for from God. Then they look at their own helplessness, and condemnation overwhelms them.

Let me bare my soul to you on this matter of unanswered prayers. First of all, I respect and love all the teachers and ministers of faith and positive confession. They are great men and women of God. We desperately need to be reminded of the power of faith and proper thinking. It is all very much scriptural, and those who resist or deny such teaching have probably never taken the time to hear what is truly being taught. But there is one major problem: The faith bandwagon is rolling along, full speed, on wheels that are not balanced. And if it keeps rolling in the direction it is now going, without balance, it will get sidetracked, and many trusting people will get hurt. Already some are giving up, because they have come under bondage to teachings on faith, which suggest all unanswered prayers are a result of human error. In other words, if it didn't work for you, you did something wrong; so keep doing it until you get it right.

You cannot feed your faith only on self-serving promises of healing, wealth, success, and prosperity, any more than you can grow healthy and strong eating only desserts. Faith comes by hearing "all the Word," not just preferred portions.

What about Bible truths that speak of suffering that teaches obedience? As Jesus did, we learn obedience by the things we suffer (Hebrews 5:8). There are as many Scriptures about suffering as there are about faith.

Our faith should not be afraid to investigate Bible passages that deal with God's delays, His seasons of silence, and even His sovereignty—the times when He acts without giving man an explanation.

Peter warned that faith should not stand alone. He said, ". . . add to your faith virtue; and to virtue knowledge; And to knowledge temperance; and to temperance patience . . ." (2 Peter 1:5, 6). Faith without patience and virtue and self-control (temperance) becomes self-centered and unbalanced.

All diseases are not caused by demons or evil spirits. Most are caused by a lack of self-control, gluttony, or bad habits. This belching, bloated generation stuffs itself on mountains of junk food, desserts, and poisoned beverages; then, when our bodies are weakened and stricken with disease, in panic, we run to God's Word, for a quick panacea. We will do anything to be healed—except practice self-control. And even though God, in His mercy, will often overrule our self-indulgent ways and heal our bodies, we need to invest our faith in some self-control.

There are times, in the Bible, when God could not, or did not, answer—no matter how many times it was asked for—no matter how great the faith or how positive the confession. Paul was not delivered from the affliction that buffeted him, though he prayed diligently for an answer. "For this thing I besought the Lord thrice, that it might depart from me" (2 Corinthians 12:8).

First, God wanted to see the work of grace completed in Paul. He would not permit His child to become puffed up with pride. He would not rejoice in a deliverance, but in learning how God's power could be his in times of weakness. But look what it worked out in Paul, proving God was right in not answering his request:

> . . . Most gladly therefore will I rather glory in my
> infirmities, that the power of Christ may rest upon me.
> Therefore I take pleasure in infirmities, in reproaches, in
> necessities, in persecutions, in distresses for Christ's
> sake: for when I am weak, then am I strong.
>
> 2 Corinthians 12:9, 10

Was Paul lacking in faith? full of negative thoughts? wrong confession? Why didn't Paul preach the message we hear so much today: "You don't have to suffer infirmities, poverty, distresses, suffering. You don't have to put up with necessity or weakness. Claim your victory over all suffering and pain . . ."?

Paul wanted more than healing, more than success, more than deliverance from prickly thorns: He wanted Christ! Paul would rather suffer than try to overrule God. That is why he could shout, "I glory in my present situation—God is at work in me through all I suffer. In and through it all, I know my present suffering cannot be compared with the glory that awaits me."

We abuse our answers. We become ungrateful, and we so often turn our deliverance into disaster. That's what happened to Hezekiah. God sent a prophet to warn him he was to prepare to die, saying, "Thou shalt die, and not live." Hezekiah wept, repented, and begged God for an additional fifteen years. God granted his prayer. He was given a new lease on life. The very first year into his reprieve, he compromised, exposing Israel to the enemy kings. He brought disaster upon his family and his nation.

There are other times when God refuses to answer our prayer requests, because He has a better way. He will answer, all right, but we will not recognize it as such. We will see it as rejection, but, through it all, God will be doing His perfect will. You find this principle at work when Israel was being led away, captive, to the land of the Chaldeans. "What a disaster," they cried. "God has rejected our prayers; we are forsaken. God has turned a deaf ear to us." Those who were left in Jerusalem became puffed up, thinking God had heard their prayers and blessed them by permitting them to stay. But those who stayed behind were totally destroyed by sword, famine, and pestilence, until they were all consumed (Jeremiah 24:10).

But those who were taken captive were told, "You have been sent out of this place into the land of the Chaldeans for your own good . . ." (*see* Jeremiah 24:5). They never did recognize God at work, preserving a remnant, but those who were "saved through suffering" were returned to rebuild the land.

Some of My Prayers Have Not Yet Been Answered

There is an old saying, "Honest confession is good for the soul." I confess to you that I have not yet received answers to two prayers I have been praying for years. Already I hear somebody say, "Brother David, don't do that! That is negative! That is a wrong confession. No wonder you haven't received those two answers yet!" I am more amused than hurt by such comments. I refuse to ignore the facts. The facts are that I have earnestly prayed about these two matters. I have laid hold of every promise in the Bible; I have confidence that God is able to do anything; I have given my blessed Lord mountain-moving faith! Yet, the years roll by, and I have not yet seen the answers. Thousands of my prayers have been answered. I see answers to my prayers every single day of my life. God does the miraculous in my behalf, at every turn in my life. But still, those two prayers have not yet been answered.

I'll let the experts on prayer and faith try to analyze the

reasons for these unanswered prayers; but, as for me, I am not one bit worried about it. I've been all through the self-condemning bit. I've had quite enough of blaming myself for not receiving the answer when I wanted it. God is bringing a balance into my faith! My positive confession is being rechanneled in the right direction. And, oh, the joy and freedom when your faith in God no longer depends on just getting answers. What a release when your faith focuses only on Jesus and receiving His holy character.

Will My Prayers Ever Be Answered?

I believe in Holy Ghost timing. In God's own time, all our prayers will be answered, in one way or another. The trouble is, we are afraid to submit our prayers to Holy Ghost scrutiny. Some of our prayers need to be purged. Some of our faith is being misspent on requests that are not mature. We are so convinced that "if our request is in accordance to His will, we should get it." We simply do not know how to pray, "Thy will be done!" We don't want His will as much as those things permitted by His will. The only test we require of our prayers is rather self-centered: "Can I find it in God's catalog of things permitted?" So we search all through God's Word and cleverly lay out all the reasons why we should be granted certain blessings and answers. We match the promises to tailor our specific requests. When we are convinced we have a good case and have garnered enough promises, we march boldly into the presence of God, as if to say, "Lord, I've got an iron-tight case—in no way can You turn me down. I've checked my faith. I've got Your Word on the matter. I've done everything according to plan. It's mine! I claim it! Right now!"

Is that all that faith is about? simply a tool to pray out of God the benefits of promises? a challenge to His faithfulness? a test of His Word? a key to unlock God's blessing room? It seems to me we are marching into God's throne room with our faith banners waving, armed with an arsenal of promises, ready to violently claim all that is due us. All the while, we picture our approving Father congratulating us on unraveling the mystery of faith and therefore entitling ourselves to the bounties of heaven.

Until God restructures our desires and ambitions, we are going to keep on squandering our precious faith on things created, rather than the Creator. How craven and corrupt our faith becomes when it is used simply to acquire things. What a tragedy that we should boast that our faith produced for us a new car, an airplane, a financial bonanza, a new home, and so forth.

Faith is a form of thought, albeit positive, divine thought. But Jesus warned us not to give one thought to material things. "Only Gentiles [heathen] seek these things" (*see* Matthew 6:32). How very clear Jesus is on this matter, saying, "Therefore. . . . Take no thought for your life, what ye shall eat, or what ye shall drink; nor yet for your body, what ye shall put on. . . . For your heavenly Father knoweth that ye have need of all these things" (Matthew 6:25, 32).

Even the wicked prosper, at times, and it can't be said that faith produced it. God rains His love and blessings on the just, as well as the unjust. Show me a prospering Christian, and I'll show you a reprobate prospering even more.

I abhor the idea of teaching Christians how to use faith to become prosperous or more successful. That runs contrary to the teaching of the lowly Nazarene who called on His followers to sell out and give to the poor. He warned against building bigger barns and deplored the consuming hunger for worldly goods. He had no time for those who stored up treasures here on earth. He taught that His children should not become entangled with the deceitfulness of riches, but that faith should cause us to set our affection on things above.

How can it be that, with all the teaching we have today about faith, Jesus should say, ". . . Nevertheless when the Son of man cometh, shall he find faith on the earth?" (Luke 18:8). Could it be Jesus does not consider the modern brand of faith to be faith at all? Is our so-called faith so self-serving that it is becoming an abomination to the Lord? No matter how many Scriptures are quoted to support it, self-serving faith is a perversion of truth.

Compare much of the materialistic faith so prevalent today with the faith described in Hebrews 11! The things hoped for by these great men and women of God could not be measured by any worldly standard. The substance they sought was not money, houses, success, or a painless life. They exercised their faith to win God's approval of their lives. Abel's faith focused only on righteousness, and God gifted him with it. Enoch's faith was so God centered that he was translated. His faith had but one single motive: to know and please God. Faith, to Noah, meant "moving with fear" to prepare for the coming judgment. How that man would weep if he could ever witness the madness of materialism, which grips our generation.

Abraham exercised his faith to keep reminding himself he was a stranger on this earth. His blessing pact on this earth produced only a tent in which to dwell, because he put all his faith in that city whose builder and maker is God.

Some who had a reputation for having great faith ". . . received not the promise" (Hebrews 11:39). Those who did obtain promises used their faith to work righteousness, to gain strength in times of weakness, and to put the enemy to chase.

Were some of them not living in faith? Did God refuse to answer some of their prayers? After all, not all these prayer and faith warriors were delivered. Not all lived to see answers to their prayers. Not all were spared pain, suffering, and even death. Some were tortured; others were torn asunder, wandering about destitute, afflicted, tormented (*see* Hebrews 11:36–39).

These were great men and women of faith, who suffered cruel mockings, beatings, and imprisonment. They were not afflicted and tormented because of a lack of faith or a wrong confession, or because they harbored a grudge or ill will. Couldn't men of faith produce more than goatskins for their backs? Couldn't they have risen up, in faith, to claim that one great promise that no plague could come near their dwelling?

Oh, my dear friend, the world was not worthy of these saints of faith, because they had the kind of faith that crushed every claim of the flesh. Their faith had a single eye; they considered all the blessings of God as eternal and spiritual, rather than earthly and now.

Yes, I know the faith chapter closes by saying, "God has provided some better thing for us . . ." (*see* Hebrews 11:40). But how shall we define that better thing God has prepared for those who have faith today? Better health benefits? Better goatskins? Better financial arrangements? Better times of ease and prosperity? Better old-age benefits? Bigger barns, filled with all we need to retire in style?

No! I say God has provided for us something better in His only begotten Son. He came to earth as man, to show us an even greater, single-minded faith; and that is "to do the will of the Father." We should be spending more time getting into Jesus than trying to get something out of Him. We should not be praying that God make things happen *for* us, but *to* us.

Those who are so exercised in their faith for healing, for financial blessings, for solutions to problems, should, instead, focus all their faith on obtaining the "rest in Christ." There is a faith that rests not in answered prayer, but in the knowledge that our Lord will do what is right for us.

Don't worry about whether God is saying, "Yes!" or, "No!"

to your request. Don't be downcast when the answer is not in sight. Quit thinking of faith formulas and methods. Just commit every prayer to Jesus and go about your business, with confidence that He will not be one moment early or late in answering. And, if the answer you seek is not forthcoming, say to your heart, "He is all I need. If I need more, He will not withhold it. He will do it in His time, in His way; and, if He does not fulfill my request, He must have a perfect reason for not doing so. No matter what happens, I will always have faith in His faithfulness."

God help us if our faith serves the creature rather than the Creator. God forgive us if we are more concerned about getting prayers answered than in learning total submission to Christ Himself. We do not learn obedience by the things we obtain, but by the things we suffer. Are you willing to learn obedience by suffering a little longer with what appears to be unanswered prayer? Will you rest in His love, while patiently waiting for the promise, after you have done all the will of the Father?

Jettison your theology, and get back to simplicity. Faith is a gift, not a diploma. Faith should not be a burden or a puzzle. The more childlike it is, the better it works. You need no seminar or textbook; you need no guide. The Holy Spirit will lead you closer to Jesus—who is the Word—by whom cometh faith.

14

Jesus and Storms

Jesus ordered His disciples into a boat that was headed for a collision. The Bible says He constrained them to get into a ship. It was headed for troubled waters; it would be tossed about like a bobbing cork. The disciples would be thrust into a mini-Titanic experience, and Jesus knew it all the time. "And straightway Jesus constrained his disciples to get into a ship, and to go before him unto the other side, while he sent the multitudes away" (Matthew 14:22).

Where was Jesus? He was up in the mountains overlooking that sea; He was there, praying for them not to fail in the test He knew they must go through. The boat trip, the storm, the tossing waves, and the winds were all a part of a trial the Father had planned. They were about to learn the greatest lesson they would ever learn. That lesson was how to recognize Jesus in the storm.

They recognized Him to this point as the Miracle Worker, the Man who turned loaves and fishes into miracle food, the Friend of sinners, the One who brought salvation to every kind of lost humanity. They knew Him as the Supplier of all their needs, even to paying their taxes from a fish's mouth.

They recognized Jesus as the Christ, the very Son of God. They knew He had the words of eternal life. They knew He had power over all the works of the devil. They knew Him as a teacher, having taught them how to pray and forgive, to bind and loose.

But they had never learned to recognize Jesus in the storm. Tragically, those disciples who thought they really knew Him best could not recognize Him when the storm hit.

That's the root of most of our trouble today. We trust Jesus for miracles and healing. We believe Him for our salvation and the forgiveness of our sins. We look to Him as the supplier of all our needs. We trust Him to bring us into glory one day. But, when a sudden storm falls upon us, and it seems as if everything is falling apart, we find it difficult to see Jesus anywhere near. We can't believe He allows storms to teach us how to trust. We are never quite sure He is nearby when things really get rough.

The ship is now tossing; it appears to be sinking; winds are blowing; they have everything going contrary to them.

> But the ship was now in the midst of the sea, tossed with waves: for the wind was contrary. And in the fourth watch of the night Jesus went unto them, walking on the sea. And when the disciples saw him walking on the sea, they were troubled, saying, It is a spirit; and they cried out for fear. But straightway Jesus spake unto them, saying, Be of good cheer; it is I; be not afraid.
>
> Matthew 14:24–27

They were so suddenly swamped, so suddenly overwhelmed; the very thought that Jesus was nearby, watching over them, was absurd. One probably said, "This is the work of Satan; the devil is out to kill us because of all those miracles we've had a part in."

Another probably said, "Where did we go wrong? Which one of us has sin in his life? Let's have a heart searching; let's confess one to another. God is mad at somebody on this boat!"

Another could have said, "Why us? We're doing what He said to do. We're obedient. We're not out of God's will. Why all of a sudden this storm? Why would God allow us to be shaken up so much, on a divine mission?"

In their darkest hour, Jesus went to them. How difficult it must have been for Jesus to wait on the edge of that storm, loving them so much, feeling every pain they felt, wanting so much to keep them from getting hurt, yearning after them as a father for his children in trouble. Yet, He knew they could never fully know Him or trust Him, until the full fury of the storm was upon them. He would reveal Himself only when they had reached the limit of their faith. The boat would never have gone down, but their fear would have drowned them more quickly than the waves beating on the ship. The only fear of drowning was that of drowning from despair, fear, and anxiety—not water.

Remember, Jesus can calm that sea at any time, simply by speaking the word, but the disciples cannot. Could faith on their part have been exercised? Could not they command the sea in Jesus' name? ("Greater works shall ye do.") Could not the promises have been put into practice? ("All things asked in prayer . . . ye shall have!") These cannot happen until we have learned to recognize Jesus in the storm, have received faith to ride out the storm, and have learned to be of good cheer when the boat appears to be sinking.

When the disciples saw Jesus, they thought it was a spirit, a ghost. They did not recognize Jesus in that storm. They saw a ghost, an apparition. The thought of Jesus being so near, so much a part of what they were going through, did not even enter their minds.

The Greatest Danger

Here is the danger we all face: not being able to see Jesus in our troubles—instead we see ghosts. In that peak moment

of fear when the night is the blackest, the storm is the an-
griest, the winds are the loudest, and the hopelessness the
most overwhelming, Jesus always draws near to us, to reveal
Himself as the Lord of the flood, the Saviour in storms. "The
Lord sitteth upon the flood; yea, the Lord sitteth King for
ever" (Psalms 29:10).

The disciples compounded their fears. Now, not only were
they afraid of the storm, they had a new fear: ghosts. The
storm was spewing up ghosts; mysterious spirits were on the
loose.

You would think at least one disciple would have recognized what was happening and said, "Look friends, Jesus said
He would never leave us or forsake us. He sent us on this
mission; we are in the center of His will. He said the steps of a
righteous man are ordered by Himself. Look again. That's our
Lord! He's right here! He's never been far away. We've never
once been out of His sight. Everything's under control."

But not one disciple could recognize Him. They did not
expect Him to be in their storm. They expected Him at the
Samaritan well. They expected Him to be there with outstretched arms, bidding little children to come. They expected Him to be in the temple, driving out the money
changers. And they expected Him to one day be at the right
hand of the Father, to make them kings and priests. But never,
never did they expect Him to be with them, or even near
them, in a storm!

It was, to them, just an act of destiny; an unexpected disaster; a tragic accident of fate; an unwanted, unexpected, un-
necessary trial; a lonely, fearful journey into darkness and
despair. It was a night to be forgotten!

God saw that storm through different eyes. It was as much a
test for these disciples as the wilderness was for Jesus. God
took them away from the miracles, shut them up in a tiny, frail
boat, far from the upper room, then turned nature loose. God
allowed them to be shaken but not sunken.

The Greatest Lesson

There was only one lesson to be learned, only one. It was a simple lesson, not some deep, mystical, earth-shattering one. Jesus simply wanted to be trusted as their Lord, in every storm of life. He simply wanted them to maintain their cheer and confidence, even in the blackest hours of trial. That's all.

Jesus did not want them to conjure up ghosts; but they did, just as we all still do. Jesus must have appeared as twelve different ghosts in the twelve separate minds of those disciples.

Perhaps one thought to himself, "I know that ghost; that's the ghost of lying. I lied a few weeks back. That's what this storm is all about. That's the reason we're in trouble: I lied. That's the ghost of lying trying to warn me to quit lying. I will! I will! Just get me out of this mess, and I'll quit lying."

Another probably thought, "That's the ghost of hypocrisy! I'm two-faced. I'm a phony. Now I can see what I am in this storm. That's why the storm. God sent that ghost to warn me to straighten up. I will! I will! I will! No more hypocrisy! Just please deliver me!"

Another: "That's the ghost of compromise. I've been compromising lately. Oh, my. I've really failed the Lord. It's been a secret thing I tried to hide, but I'm scared now. You allowed this storm; You sent that ghost to warn me to get back to holiness. I will! I will! Just give me another chance."

Another: "That's the ghost of covetousness. I've been too materialistic."

Another: "That's the ghost of wasted time. I've grown lazy. I've not been witnessing. I've grown cold, lukewarm, but now I've learned my lesson!"

Another: "That's the ghost of grudges. I've not been forgiving as I should. I've been avoiding certain people. That's why God is shaking me up, to teach me to quit holding grudges."

Another: "That's the ghost of secret sin; evil thoughts. I

can't seem to give them up, so God had to send this storm to expose me."

Another: "That's the ghost of broken promises. I promised God I'd do this thing, and I didn't do it. Now God is getting back at me. He's mad at me, so He put me out in this storm. I'm sorry. That's the lesson; I've learned my lesson!"

No! No! A thousand times no! Those are all ghosts of our own minds, apparitions only. None of these are the real lessons to be learned. God is not mad at you. You are not in a storm because you failed. These ghosts are not even in your storm.

It is Jesus at work, seeking to reveal Himself in His saving, keeping, preserving power! He is wanting you to know the storm has one purpose only—and that is to bring you to complete rest and trust in His power and presence at all times, in the middle of miracles and in the middle of storms. It is so easy, in a storm, to lose a sense of His presence and feel we are left alone, to battle against hopeless odds; or that somewhere along the line, as a result of sin or compromise, Christ has forsaken us and left us out there, all alone, in that tossing boat.

What about those times when the contrary winds are sickness, disease, and pain? What about when cancer strikes? What about when pain and fear are so overwhelming, you can't spare a thought about the closeness of Jesus? Your sudden storm is upon you, and there is no other thought that survival. You don't want to die; you want to live. You see the ghost of death in the shadows, and you tremble. You don't have the strength to face even the next hour.

 That is what the presence of Jesus is all about. It is a revelation that is the most powerful when it comes to us at that most-needed time.

15

The Ultimate Healing

Resurrection from the dead is the "ultimate healing." I tried to share that glorious truth with the grieving parents of a five-year-old boy who had died, just hours before, of leukemia. They had begged God for the healing of their dear child. The whole church prayed earnestly. Friends had prophesied: "He will not die; he will be healed." One week prior to the little boy's death, the heartbroken father picked up the fevered child and walked him around the room. "God, I'll not give him up. Your promises are true. My faith has never faltered. More than two or three have agreed in Your name that he should be healed. I confess it now, and I claim it." In spite of everything, the child died.

I was there when that child was laid out in a tiny casket. I looked, with horror, on all those sad faces of Christian friends who had gathered to mourn his death. The parents were in a state of shock. Everybody was afraid to speak out what they were thinking. I know the church people were thinking it, and the pastor acted as if he was thinking it. I know the parents were certainly thinking it. And just what was this unthinkable thought gripping their minds? Simply this: *God did not answer prayer! Someone goofed! Someone stood in the way of God's healing power! Someone is responsible for this child's death, because of a grudge, a hidden motive, or a secret sin. Someone or something hindered the healing.*

It was there and then that a glorious truth dawned on me, and I took the parents aside and briefly unburdened my heart, "Don't question God," I said. "Your prayers have all been answered. God gave your son the ultimate healing. That little, fevered, diseased body has been abandoned; and Ricky is right now clothed in his perfect, painless body. Ricky has been healed! God did exceedingly above all you could ask or think of Him. He is alive and well—all that has changed is his body and his location!"

Those parents turned on me with anger. They were bitter and confused, and they left the graveside to enter a bleak five-year period of doubts, questions, guilt, and self-examination. During that time, they would hardly speak to me. But God, in His mercy, always breaks through to sincere hearts. One day, while in prayer, the Holy Spirit came upon that grieving mother, reminding her of my message. She began praising the Lord, saying, "Ricky was healed. God did answer our prayers. Lord, forgive our doubts. Ricky is right now alive and well and enjoying his healing."

I treasure the moment we stood together, arms entwined, thanking the Lord for such comfort. Ricky's father confessed, "Dave, we were so angry with you. We thought you were heartless, suggesting our son, who had just died, had been healed. Now we understand. We were so selfish; we could not understand what was best for our son. We thought only of our own pain, our grief, our suffering. But now the Lord has shown us that Ricky was not destroyed by death, but the Lord drew him to Himself."

The Life Is Not in the Shell

These mortal bodies of ours are but mere shells, and the life is not in the shell. The shell is not for keeping, but a temporary confine that enshrouds an ever-growing, ever-maturing life force. The body is a shell that acts as a transient guardian of the life inside. The shell is synthetic in comparison to the eternal life it clothes.

Every true Christian has been imbued with eternal life. It is planted as a constantly maturing seed in our mortal bodies. It is, within us, an ever-growing, ever-expanding process of development; and it must eventually break out of the shell, to become a new form of life. This glorious life of God in us exerts pressure on the shell, and, at the very moment resurrection life is mature, the shell breaks. The artificial bonds are broken, and, like a newborn baby chick, the soul is freed from its prison. Praise the Lord!

Death is but a mere breaking of the fragile shell. At the precise moment our Lord decides our shell has served its purpose, a sudden rush of eternal life floods the soul, and God opens the shell—only to free the new creature that has come of age.

As life itself abandons the shell, after it has fulfilled its function, so must God's people abandon their old, corrupt bodies made from the dust from which they came. Who would think of picking up the fragmented pieces of shell and forcing the newborn chick back into its original state? And who would think of asking a departed loved one to give up his new, glorified body—made in Christ's own image—and return to the decaying shell from which he broke free?

To Die Is Gain?

Paul said it: "To die is gain"! (Philippians 1:21). That kind of talk is absolutely foreign to our modern spiritual vocabularies. We have become such life worshipers, that we have very little desire to depart to be with the Lord.

Paul said, "For I am in a strait betwixt two, having a desire to depart, and to be with Christ; which is far better" (Philippians 1:23). Yet, for the sake of edifying the converts, he thought it best to "stay in the shell." Or, as he put it, "live in the flesh" (v. 22).

Was Paul morbid? Did he have an unhealthy fixation with death? Did Paul show a lack of respect for the life God had blessed him with? Absolutely not! Paul lived life to the fullest. To him, life was a gift, and he had used it well to fight a good fight. He had overcome the fear of the "sting of death" and could now say, "It's better to die and be with the Lord than to stay in the flesh."

Those who die in the Lord are the winners; we who remain are the losers. How tragic that God's people still look upon the departed as losers—poor, miserable souls, cheated out of a greater measure of life. Oh! But if our spiritual eyes and ears could be opened but for a few moments, we would see our dear, loved ones on God's side of the universe, walking in the pure, crystal river of eternal life, trying to shout at us, "I won! I won! I'm free at last! Press on, dear earthlings; there is nothing to fear. Death does not sting. It is true: It is better to depart and to be with the Lord."

Did someone you love break out of his shell? Were you there when it happened? Or did the news reach you by phone or telegram? What kind of horrifying feeling rushed through your mind when you were told, "He is dead!" or "She is dead!"?

Certainly it is natural to mourn and weep for those who die. Even the death of the righteous is painful for those left behind. But, as followers of the Christ who holds the keys of death in His hand, we dare not think of death as an accident perpetuated by the devil. Satan cannot destroy a single child of God. Satan, though permitted to touch Job's flesh and afflict his body, could not take his life. God's children always die right on His schedule, not one second too soon or too late. If the steps of a righteous person are ordered by the Lord, He orders the final one, too.

Death is not the ultimate healing: Resurrection is! Death is the passage, and sometimes that passage can be painful, even excruciating. I have seen many of God's chosen people die in tremendous pain. But Paul answers that well by proclaiming "For I reckon that the sufferings of this present time are not worthy to be compared with the glory which shall be revealed in us" (Romans 8:18). No matter how much pain and suffering wreak havoc on these bodies, it is not even worthy to be compared with the unspeakable glory that awaits those who endure the passage.

God's Magnetic Pull

In my years of watching the body die, I have noted one common experience. I call it "the magnetic pull." I'm convinced that death comes to the saint long before the last breath is taken. When the Lord turns the key, an irreversible magnetic pull of God's Spirit begins to draw the loved one to Himself. Somehow, God permits that person who is being drawn to know it is happening. He is given an inner knowledge that he is going home. He has already seen a bit of the heavenly glory. While loved ones gather around him to plead for his resurrection, you can sense he doesn't want to stay imprisoned in his shell any longer. A crack has appeared; he has peered through and has glimpsed the New Jerusalem, with all its exciting eternal joys. He has seen a vision of the glories awaiting him. To turn back would be emptiness.

Recently, I stood by the bedside of a saintly mother who was dying of cancer. Her hospital room was aglow with God's holy presence. Her husband and children were softly singing hymns; and, as weak as she was, she lifted her face heavenward and whispered, "I feel His pull. It's true, He does draw us to Himself. It feels like a powerful magnet, and I'm going faster and faster, and I don't want anybody to stop me, now." Within hours, she broke through her fleshy shell, into God's inner circle. In that holy hour, no one dared interfere with this divine process of changing, when the terrestrial was being swallowed up by the celestial.

It's so sad to hear Christians condemn God for taking their loved ones from them. "Lord, it's just not fair," they argue. Though it is difficult to condemn what people say in times of deep grief, I believe such questioning can be selfish. We think only of our loss, and not their gain. God only plucks out of this world those He can no longer love at a distance. The mutual love of God and the believer demands that he be in His presence. It is then love is perfected. To be with the Lord is to experience His love in its fullness.

So you stand helplessly by, as your loved one enters that passage called death. You know it's a dark, lonely path, and you can hold that hand only so far. The time comes when you have to let that loved one go and let Jesus take him by the hand. He is no longer yours; he belongs to Him. You feel so helpless, but there is not one thing you can do, but rest in the knowledge that the Lord has taken over and that your loved one is in good hands. Then, in a moment, he is out of sight. The battle is over. Only the broken shell remains. The delivered soul has taken flight into God's holy presence. The death of the righteous is a precious thing. David, the Psalmist, wrote, "Precious in the sight of the Lord is the death of his saints" (Psalms 116:15). God looks upon the death of one of His children as a cherished moment. But we humans find little or nothing to cherish in this experience.

A young mother told me a pitiful story of the trauma she endured after the death of her two children. The first child died at the age of eighteen months. The second lived only about two months. She had thought God had given her the second child to make up for the loss of the first—now both were dead. She and her Christian husband went through months of self-examination. Was there sin in their lives? Had they angered God by doubting His healing power? Were they in some way responsible for the deaths of their children? Then, one dark day, a "good Christian friend" came to them with what she declared to be a message from the Lord. They were, she said, being chastised by the Lord for hidden grudges and dishonesty in their marriage. "Those children would still be alive," they were told, "if your hearts had been purged of sin and if your confession had been right."

They were crushed to despair. But God, in His mercy, showed them how ridiculous such thoughts were. Such teaching is tragic nonsense. God doesn't play Russian roulette with lives!

Shall we quit praying for the dying? Shall we give up on the terminally ill? Should we just lie down and die, if that is ultimate healing? Never! More than ever in my life, I believe in divine healing. We should pray for everybody to be healed. And the only people who are not healed, according to our concept of healing, are those who are chosen for His ultimate healing. Some are not given restored organs or limbs; instead, they are given the perfect healing: glorified, painless, eternal bodies. What is there that our minds can conceive as being a greater miracle than resurrection from the dead?

We Are Too Earthbound

Any message about death bothers us. We try to ignore even thinking about it. We suspect those who talk about it of being morbid. Occasionally we will talk about what heaven must be like, but, most of the time, the subject of death is taboo.

How different the first Christians were! Paul spoke much about death. In fact, our resurrection from the dead is referred to in the New Testament as our "blessed hope." But, nowadays death is considered an intruder that cuts us off from the good life we have been accustomed to. We have so cluttered our lives with material things; we are bogged down with life. The world has trapped us with materialism. We can no longer bear the thought of leaving our beautiful homes, our lovely things, our charming sweethearts. We seem to be thinking, "To die now would be too great a loss. I love the Lord, but I need time to enjoy my real estate. I'm married. I've yet to prove my oxen. I need more time."

Have you noticed there is very little talk, nowadays, about heaven or about leaving this old world behind? Instead, we are bombarded with messages on how to use our faith to acquire more things. "The next revival," said one such well-known teacher, "will be a financial revival. God is going to pour out financial blessings on all believers."

What a stunted concept of God's eternal purposes! No wonder so many Christians are frightened by the thought of death. The truth is, we are far from understanding Christ's call to forsake the world and all its entanglements. He calls us to come and die, to die without building memorials to ourselves, to die without worrying how we should be remembered. Jesus left no autobiography, no headquarters complex, no university or Bible college. He left nothing to perpetuate His memory but the bread and the wine.

What is the greatest revelation of faith, and how is it to be exercised? You will find it in Hebrews:

> These all died in faith . . . confessing that they were strangers and pilgrims on the earth. . . . But now they desire a better country, that is, an heavenly: wherefore God is not ashamed to be called their God: for he hath prepared for them a city.
>
> *See* Hebrews 11:13, 16

Here is my honest prayer to God:

Lord, help me cut loose from the bondage of things. Let me not squander my gift of life on my own selfish pleasures and goals. Help me to bring all my appetites under Your control. Make me remember I am a pilgrim, not a settler. I am not Your fan, but Your follower. Most of all, deliver me from the bondage of the fear of death. Make me finally understand that to die in Christ is gain. Help me to look forward, with precious anticipation, to my moment of ultimate healing.

I am he that liveth, and was dead; and, behold, I am alive for evermore. . . .

Revelation 1:18

. . . through death he might destroy him that had the power of death, that is, the devil; And deliver them who through fear of death were all their lifetime subject to bondage.

Hebrews 2:14, 15

But is now made manifest by the appearing of our Saviour Jesus Christ, who hath abolished death, and hath brought life and immortality to light through the gospel.

2 Timothy 1:10